A MAGNOLIA ADVENTURE

THE RED STILETTO BOOKCLUB SERIES

ANNE-MARIE MEYER

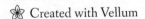

To My Family

1

PENNY

I loved the clicking sound that keyboards made as people typed. It meant that words were being written and stories were being told. I wasn't sure how many times I would pull my attention from the spreadsheets on my computer and lean back, just so I could listen to Victoria and Tracy, our new reporter, type their stories.

Our first edition, Magnolia Move-ins, had been a hit. It sold out the first two days after launching. The success only helped me confirm I was where I needed to be. Magnolia. Magnolia Daily. This was my life.

It took me so many decades to get to this point, but now that I was experiencing what pure bliss was, I was grateful for the road I took to be here. I was finally home.

"Morning, Spencer." Victoria's voice turned my attention to my office door.

My heart picked up speed as I waited for my

boyfriend to appear. I felt like a young girl, thinking those words, but it was true. Spencer and I were dating. And I couldn't be happier.

I was already out of my seat when he appeared in the doorway. I wrapped my arms around him as soon as he was close enough for me to hug him. He chuckled as he buried his face in the hollow of my neck and took in a deep breath.

We scooted out of view of Victoria and Tracy. Once I was certain they couldn't see us, I kissed him. His lips were on mine, and we moved like we were two teenagers hiding from our parents.

I loved kissing this man. He completed me in a way that I didn't think was possible. We were meant to be together. I loved him.

"I just saw you this morning," Spencer said when he finally pulled away.

I groaned as he stepped back. I didn't want him to stop kissing me. I wanted to remain like this forever. "It's been that long?" I asked as I readjusted my shirt since it'd wrinkled from our embrace.

He nodded.

"I just can't get enough of you," I said with a wink as I moved to sit down at my desk. Spencer dropped into the chair across from my desk and scrubbed his face.

I winced when I saw that my red lipstick was all over his mouth. I reached forward and grabbed a tissue from the box on my desk. "Sorry," I whispered.

He chuckled as he moved to wipe his lips. "Hazard of the job, I guess."

I nodded and then leaned back in my chair, bouncing a few times as I studied him. "Did I forget something at home?" I asked.

His gaze was focused on the tissue that he was now folding smaller and smaller. "I just wanted to let you know that I'm not mad."

My chest felt heavy as the argument we had last night came rushing back to me. Even though he'd said he was over it this morning, I could tell that it had bothered him. Ever since Maggie gave me the addresses of his daughters, he'd shut me out of that part of his life.

He told me that it was something he was going to have to conquer on his own, and I tried to be understanding. I did. But the holidays were coming up, and I'd wanted to know if I should plan for more people at the table.

He got upset and told me that I was pushing—which I was. I feared that Spencer was just going to keep sitting on this without actually doing anything. Having had a strained relationship with my own daughter, I realized how precious time was. A commodity that I couldn't control and one I couldn't get back.

I feared that he would regret taking his time like this.

"I'm sorry for pushing you again," I said with a soft smile. I wanted him to know that I was willing to follow his timeline—with a few gentle nudges from me.

He nodded, but it didn't detract from the serious

expression on his face. He wanted to talk further about this, so I pinched my lips.

"I know you want the girls to come to Thanksgiving, and at first, it hurt." His voice grew quiet, and my heart ached for him.

He spent so much of his life running from his past, and here I was, forcing him to face it. I knew it was painful, but I also knew he would feel an undeniable freedom once he accepted and faced the parts that made his heart ache.

He would feel more complete if he rebuilt his relationships with his daughters. At least, that was my hope.

"Rosalie was the one who always planned our holiday get-togethers. So, when you brought it up..." His voice drifted off, and I could see the heartbreak in his gaze.

I wanted to jump in and tell him that I was sorry. But I didn't. Instead, I kept quiet even though I was aching inside. I wanted to take away his pain, but I knew that was impossible.

"It was hard to think about doing something without her."

"I know," I whispered.

He grew quiet, and I could tell that he was choosing his words. "But I know she would be disappointed in me for how I've treated the girls. I should have never let our relationship get this stale. I should have stuck it out." His voice cracked, so he waited a minute before continuing. "I should have fought for them."

Tears were brimming my eyes, and all I could do was nod. I knew that he was broken; I could see it in his eyes. But there was nothing I could do to fix his past. All I could do was love him while he worked to fix his future.

"I think I want to go to Harmony Island to find Abigail and Sabrina."

I paused. This was the first time I'd heard him say their names. I already knew them because of Maggie's detective skills, but to hear him say them meant his decision to see them was real.

"Are you sure?" I asked, shifting in my seat. I was equally nervous and excited for him.

Spencer nodded. "I am." Then he furrowed his brow. "Will you come with me?"

I couldn't fight the smile that emerged on my lips. I nodded slowly. "If that's what you want, I'd be honored to go with you."

He blew out his breath as if he were attempting to blow out the stress. "I want that." Then his worried lips tipped up into an irresistible smile. "I want you."

My entire body flushed. My heart pounded as desire rose up inside of me. We'd both decided to take this relationship slow, but it was becoming more and more apparent that he was a man and I was a woman. I was ready to be reminded of that.

"Hush," I whispered as I peered over at Victoria and Tracy. If they heard, they didn't move to acknowledge it. I knew it was probably impossible for them to hear what we were talking about unless they'd suddenly obtained Super-man-like hearing. But still, prudence was the name of the game for me.

"So, when do you want to head out?" I asked as I threaded my fingers together and set my hands down on my desk.

"When can you take time off?"

I scoffed. Victoria was the go-getter I needed. I doubted she would be sad to hear that I needed to take a few days off. At times, I wondered if I got in her way. She took every story, every aspect of this newspaper, by the horns and corralled it into submission. This place was running like a well-oiled machine, and it wasn't because of me.

"I doubt I will have to fight Victoria about me taking some time off." I shrugged. "So, whenever you are ready, I'll let her know."

Spencer cleared his throat. "Tomorrow?"

"Tomorrow?" For some reason, my chest tightened. Perhaps it was because the reality of what was going to happen came crashing into me. I was going to be meeting his daughters. I was going to help him heal from the trauma he was carrying around.

That was a big task. One that I was starting to worry I would be unable to carry out.

"Will that work?" Spencer asked, pulling me from my thoughts.

I contemplated saying no. That I needed a day or so to

process this. But I didn't. This wasn't about me. This was about him. "Sure," I said, and then the tone of my voice carried to my own ears, and I realized how uncertain I sounded. So, I followed it with a determined, "Yes."

Spencer looked visibly relieved as he smiled and nodded. Then he sighed. "It'll be work, but with you next to me, I think I can conquer it."

I smiled. I wanted him to rely on me. This was what I missed about relationships and what I'd spent my whole life running from. And now that I was presented with it, I ran toward it at full speed.

I was ready to depend on him and have him depend on me. "You'll do great."

We made small talk for the next few minutes. I could see Spencer's fear lessen and his confidence grow, which only made me more excited for him. By the time he moved to go, he was actually smiling. His dimple on his left side deepened, which made me happy. I knew when that showed up, he was truly happy.

"I'll see you tonight?" he asked as he moved around the desk and wrapped his hands around my waist.

My heart pounded. It always made me feel feminine and small when he touched me. I nodded. "I'll help Victoria wrap up this next edition, and then I'll be home. Maybe we can go to the inn and eat with Maggie since we'll be leaving?"

Ever since Maggie told me that she and Archer were trying for a baby, I'd been worried about her with each negative pregnancy test. She was trying to remain positive, but I knew she was hurting. If I could conjure up a positive test for her, I'd do it.

Unfortunately, I lacked that ability.

Spencer kissed my nose. "Of course."

I smiled and slipped my hands from his shoulders up to the nape of his neck. He responded by pulling me close.

"Thanks for loving me," he whispered as he buried his face in my neck.

I smiled, reveling in the feeling of his body pressed to mine. The feeling of warmth that I always got when I held him.

"I love you," I whispered.

"I love you, too."

It took a minute before we let each other go. Spencer cleared his throat, threw me a wave, and headed out of my office. As he opened the door, Victoria hurried in.

"Afternoon, Spencer," she said as she zeroed in on me. She had a clipboard in hand, and I prepared myself for whatever she wanted to discuss—which was most likely everything.

Spencer just chuckled, said goodbye, and left.

With my distraction now gone, I turned my focus to Victoria, who didn't miss a beat and was already hammering me with all her questions.

I settled down on my chair and gave her my full attention. Tomorrow, I would worry about Spencer and his daughters, but for now, I would focus on the paper.

AT SEVEN, Spencer and I pulled into the last parking spot at the inn. Thankfully, I had enough forethought to text Maggie after my three-hour long meeting with Victoria just to let her know that we were coming. She'd texted back that she'd save us a table, and I'd sent her one of those heart emojis that turned into lots of hearts when you opened the text.

I was excited to tell my daughter about our plans to head to Harmony Island. I had a feeling she would be equally excited. With the lack of a baby on the way, she threw herself into everything else. All in an effort to keep her mind off what she felt she was missing out on.

Spencer gestured for me to wait and then climbed out of his seat. I unbuckled my seatbelt and watched as he rounded the hood and pulled open my door. His hand appeared, ready to take mine and help me out.

My lips tipped up into a smile. Spencer seemed rough around the edges, but he was a gentleman through and through. I felt so lucky that I'd found a man who treated me this way.

The inn was bustling when we walked through the front door. Guests were either moving around the first floor or sitting in the living room, reading and talking. I'd never seen this place booming like this. My heart swelled. My daughter had worked so hard for this, and I couldn't have been prouder.

She'd brought so much happiness back to this small town and to me. I just wanted the best for her.

"Hey, Mom." Maggie appeared in front of me. Her cheeks were pink, and she looked tired but happy.

We hugged, and I gave her an extra squeeze. I wanted her to know that I loved her and was here for her.

"It's busy tonight," I said once she pulled back.

She tucked her hair behind her ear and nodded. "Yeah. I can't believe it."

I smiled as I scanned the room. Maggie had come here with the intent of helping me sell the inn to fund her interior design business, but now, it had become something different. People were changed when they came here, and Maggie was the one who started it all.

"It looks amazing in here," Spencer said. He was scanning the different rooms we could see from where we were standing.

Everything was decorated for fall. Pumpkins sat on every surface. Garlands of leaves were draped along the fireplace mantle and around the banister. It looked beautiful.

"I can't wait to see what you do for Christmas," I said as I turned my attention back to my daughter and gave her an approving smile.

Maggie smiled back. "I have lots of plans."

I reached out and squeezed her hand. "I'm sure you do."

She showed us to our table, tucked in the back corner

of the dining room. There was a *reserved* sign in the middle, which she took away. "I'm going to let Brett know you guys are here. He's been wanting to test some new dishes on friends before he puts them on the menu. I hope that's okay."

Spencer unfolded his napkin and placed it on his lap. "Bring it on."

Maggie didn't wait. She left the table before I could ask her to sit. When we were brought our waters, it was by a local kid named Tyler. I must have been worrying my lips as I glanced around the room, because Spencer was suddenly holding my hand and attempting to catch my eye.

"You okay?" he asked.

I studied him, contemplating if I should tell him, and then shook that thought from my head. Spencer was my companion. I needed to be honest with him if we were going to make this relationship work.

"I'm just worried about Maggie, that's all," I said, emotions choking my throat.

Spencer glanced around the room before he met my gaze once more. "She'll be okay. Archer takes good care of her."

I nodded, knowing that what he was saying was true, but that did nothing for the pit that had formed in my stomach. "I know, but she's just so vulnerable. What if all of this work is what is causing her struggle to get pregnant?" I could feel the panic start to rise inside of me. I wanted to fix this for my daughter. I wanted to make it right.

"I'm sure she's fine. She's a healthy woman. When Rosalie and I were trying for Abigail, it took a few months." He patted my hand with his free one. "Sometimes, these things take time."

I nodded, knowing that what he was saying was true but struggling to fully accept it.

Thankfully, Brett appeared with two plates of what looked like creamy linguine Alfredo, and hunger overtook my worries. Spencer and I ate in silence. The food was so good that all thought left my mind and all I could focus on was eating.

By the time Maggie found us again, our plates were empty and our stomachs full. Life seemed easier to process when I wasn't hungry.

"How was Brett's lobster Alfredo?" Maggie asked as she sat down next to me.

I kissed the tips of my fingers like an Italian chef. "Amazing," I whispered.

"Yeah. He made some for Archer and me, and I about fell out of my chair while I was eating it." She patted her stomach. "I may need to buy bigger clothes if he keeps cooking like this." Then she winced, and I wondered if the same thought had entered her mind. The idea of having to buy new clothes for pregnancy instead of just weight gain.

I reached out and patted her hand. "Spencer and I are

headed to North Carolina tomorrow," I said, hoping to shift her attention to something else.

Maggie moved her gaze from me to Spencer and then back. "Really?"

She knew where Abigail and Sabrina lived. She'd found their addresses.

I nodded. "We're going to find Spencer's daughters.

Her smile warmed my soul. "That's great news," she said as she glanced over at Spencer. "It may seem hard, but it'll be worth it."

Tears filled my eyes as I thought about what she said. It was so true. Fixing a broken relationship was worth all the pain and heartache. "You'll be okay without me here?" I asked. Was it wrong that I wanted her to say no? That she needed me and wanted me to stay?

She smiled and shook her head. "I'll be fine. I've got Archer and the inn to keep me busy."

My stomach dropped a bit at her words. I knew she was trying to be strong, but I didn't want her to pretend. Pain had a way of finding you again. It never really stayed away like one would hope.

"Call me if you need me. I'll come right home."

Maggie met my gaze and then nodded. "I will." Then she turned to Spencer. "Good luck. I want to hear all about it when you bring my mom safely home."

Spencer gave her a salute, and she moved to stand. After a long hug, she pulled back. "Love you, Ma," she said.

I patted her hand. "I love you, too. When I get back, let's go shopping over the bridge."

"Sounds good."

We didn't see much of Maggie the rest of the night. After dessert, I was stuffed and tired, so Spencer and I stood and pushed in our chairs. I managed to give Maggie a quick wave as we left. She was standing at the reception desk, talking to a guest. She gave me a nod but didn't break from her conversation.

Spencer led me out the door, and once we were on the gravel leading to the parking lot, his hand found mind.

"You okay?" he asked as he peered down at me.

I wanted to say no—because that was the truth. But stressing about something that I had no control over wasn't healthy. So, I just smiled and wrapped my free hand around his arm and drew myself close to him.

"I'll be fine," I whispered.

That was all I could offer. I was going to be fine. Regardless of what the future held for Spencer or Maggie, I was going to be fine.

I had to be.

2

NAOMI

Walker had changed.

It had been a month since he came to Magnolia and whisked me away, and I couldn't believe that I'd ever entertained the thought that life would be better without him. Especially since my pregnancy had been progressing beautifully. My morning sickness was lessening, and I was starting to feel more and more like my old self—which was a relief.

We were unable to find a place in Wilmington, so we'd ended up on a small island just off the coast called Harmony Island. It was a small, quaint town which was perfect for what Walker and I wanted to do.

Start over.

The early morning breeze brushed over me as I stretched out my legs and rested them on the railing in front of me. The smell of salt and the cool temperature brought me to sip my steaming mug of apple cider. Fall was in the air, and it was my favorite time of year.

I couldn't believe that I'd gone from completely stressed and hurt—both physically and mentally—to feeling completely at home. My accident had become a distant memory.

I'd been going to see a physical therapist since I got here, and I was regaining mobility that I'd thought would be forever gone. My joints still ached, but it had dulled to a more manageable pain.

Walker was good at helping me around the house on those occasions when my pain came screaming back, but those episodes were becoming few and far between. It felt like life was returning to normal, and I was ready for that.

Especially since Jackson hadn't called me since I left.

An all too familiar ache rose up in my chest, and I rubbed my rib cage in an effort to dispel it. I hated that I'd hurt my brother. After all, he'd always been my protector, and I wanted to make him proud. But not when he felt like he could attack my fiancé and the father of my child.

Jackson was going to have to grow up someday. When he was ready to apologize, I would be willing to hear it. Until then, we were at a stalemate.

I picked up my phone that was face down on the armrest next to me and studied the screen. I had a few social media notifications and some junk email but nothing else. There were moments when I wondered if the book club ladies thought about me. Fiona had said,

"Once a Red Stiletto Book Club member, always a book club member." But I hadn't heard from any of them since I left.

I knew I shouldn't be hurt, but I couldn't help but feel a little heartbroken. After all, I did look at them as my friends. But I hadn't reached out to them either, so what right did I have to be angry with them?

"None," I whispered to no one in particular as I set my phone back down.

"Talking to yourself again?"

Walker's voice startled me. I turned to see him standing in the doorway that led out to the deck where I was sitting. His shirt was off, and his hair was tousled. He gave me a grin, and I couldn't help the warmth that filled my body.

"Good morning," I said.

He crossed the space between us and leaned down to press his lips against mine. "Morning," he said as he collapsed on the deck chair next to me.

I couldn't believe how perfect Walker was. He'd doted on me since we got here. He furnished the entire apartment within a week, making it feel like a place we could raise a family. When he wasn't at work, he was here with me, giving me more attention than he ever had.

It truly felt like a dream.

I was getting ready to tell him about the baby. I felt guilty for keeping it a secret, but I wanted the reveal to be social-media worthy—plus, I wanted to make sure that this was for real. I'd finally decided to keep it, which was a weight off my shoulders.

I wanted to make sure that Walker and I worked on our relationship before we brought a little human into the middle of us. It was selfish, but I needed to know that he was here for me as much as for the baby growing in my belly.

Pushing the guilt of keeping such a huge secret out of my mind, I turned to focus on Walker. "What do you want to do today?" I asked as I reached out and drew circles around his forearm that rested on the arm of his chair.

He glanced over at me. His expression was strange, and for a moment I wondered if I shouldn't have asked that question. It morphed into a frown before I could interpret it further, and he leaned on the arm that I was touching, effectively stopping what I was doing.

"I have to go away."

I furrowed my brow. "You do?"

He nodded. "Work needs me."

I chewed on my lip. I didn't want him to go. I wanted to spend more time with him before work took over his life like it always did. "How long are you going to be gone for?"

He leaned back in his chair and shrugged. "A week or two. Maybe a month." He glanced over at me. "Are you going to be okay without me here?" There was a hint of worry in his voice, and for a moment, I wondered if he was concerned that I would run away again.

I nodded. "I'll be fine. I'm going to try to look for a job, so I will probably be gone a lot myself." I gave him a weak smile.

Relief flooded his expression as he nodded. "Perfect."

I wasn't sure where I was even going to start looking. After all, I doubted many people wanted to hire me if I was just going to have to take time off in a few months, but I wasn't going to think about that right now. If Walker's time on the rig was starting up, I was going to need something to do while I waited for him.

Sitting around the house would be torture.

So even though I had no clue where I was going to apply, I knew that I was going to have to find something to do. Uncertainty filled my chest, but I forced a smile through it. I didn't want Walker to know that I was worried. I didn't want him to feel like he needed to stay.

I really didn't want him to worry that I was going to leave again.

Walker didn't stick around the house long. After we talked, he went and showered. I was in the kitchen getting breakfast ready when he walked in. He was dressed in a t-shirt and jeans. His hair was damp and his face freshly shaven. I smiled as my gaze drifted over him.

I was lucky. I really was. Walker had a way of stopping conversations and garnering attention when he walked into a room. I always wondered why he'd picked me. After all, he was infinitely more attractive than I was, and I felt secure enough to say that. If anything, I just felt happy that he wanted to be with me.

We ate breakfast, and Walker went to our room to pack his suitcase. I busied myself with cleaning the kitchen. When he came back out, I was wiping off the last counter.

"Well, I'm outta here," he said as he reached forward and used my hips to guide me toward him. "You going to survive without me?" He leaned forward and began kissing my neck.

I giggled and shook my head. "No." He pulled back, and I jutted out my bottom lip. "I don't want you to go."

He studied me. "I gotta go, babe. I gotta make the money." He smiled at me. "I'll be back before you know it."

I nodded and forced a smile. "I know. I was just joking."

He leaned forward and gave me a kiss. "You'll be okay without me?" He raised his eyebrows.

"I'll be perfect."

He grinned and smacked my bottom. "That's my girl."

Before I could say anything else, he let me go and grabbed his luggage. He gave me a final wave before he opened the front door and left.

I stood in the kitchen, alone, staring at the door for a few minutes. Part of me hoped that Walker would come back in and tell me that it was a mistake. That he wanted to stay here with me.

But when the door didn't open, I blew out my breath and tossed the dishcloth into the sink. I was alone again. Anxiety built up inside me as I stared around the kitchen. What was I going to do now?

Thankfully, taking a shower helped. The warm water beat against my skin, helping me feel more grounded to the world around me. I dried off, taking a moment to look at my stomach in the mirror. I was a naturally thin person, and the baby bump was more visible than it had been before.

I cupped it with my hand as tears filled my eyes. I felt bad that I was bringing a baby into a less than perfect life. It deserved so much more than I could give it. Walker and I were working well together, but I feared that it wouldn't last forever.

We still hadn't really talked about what happened to cause my accident. I tried to take responsibility for it just so we could move on, but with him gone, it was hard to not allow the fear that he'd been cheating on me to resurface.

"Don't think like that," I scolded myself.

Walker said that he'd been working, that was all. His assistant had simply forgotten. There was nothing to report. It had been a basic work trip—why wouldn't I just let it go?

So, I stopped asking, and I stopped wondering.

If I wanted to return to what we had before, I needed to keep my focus on what mattered. It didn't matter what happened in the past. My focus needed to be on the future and the baby.

I dressed, and just as I pulled a brush through my hair, there was a knock at the door. I peered from the bathroom to the front door. Was it Walker? Did he forget his keys?

Was this some elaborate plan to sweep me off my feet?

I quickly brushed some mascara on my lashes and fluffed my hair before I turned and hurried to the door.

"Did you forget—" I stopped as soon as the door swung open and saw Colten standing in front of me. "Colten?" I whispered. The pain I felt when I'd walked away from Jackson came rushing back to me. I hated the way I'd left, and I hated that I'd hurt my brother that way. "Is Jackson here?" I asked as I peered past him and down the hall.

Colten shook his head. "Can I come inside, or is he here?"

My skin pricked. "Walker isn't here. He just left for a work trip." I folded my arms, annoyed that he was acting like this. "Is there a reason you're here?"

He studied me before he pushed past me and into my apartment. I groaned, hating that he felt like he could push me around. Sure, we'd grown up together, and I was certain that he saw me as his little sister. But that didn't mean he could treat me like this.

"Hey," I said as I shut the door. "Where are you going?"

If Colten heard me, he didn't show it. He made his

way into the kitchen and plopped down on a chair next to the kitchen table. He extended his legs and rested his head in his hands behind his head. His gaze landed on me, and he didn't pull it away.

"Colten," I said as I mustered the remaining strength I had. I folded my arms and leaned my hip against the counter. I was more mobile now, but I grew tired quickly and needed support to keep from collapsing. But there was no way I wanted Colten to know that I was close to having my leg give out. I didn't want to appear weak.

"How long are you going to play this game?" he asked.

"Game? What game?"

He leaned forward, resting his arms on the table.

"How did you even find me?" I realized that he'd just shown up at my apartment.

He cleared his throat. "I have friends."

My jaw dropped. Of course. All the men in the police force were bros. "You had me followed?" I scoffed. I wanted to say that I was surprised, but the more I mulled it over, the more I began to realize that, in a way, I kind of knew this would happen. "Did Jackson ask you to do that?"

His cheeks reddened, which confused me. I raised my eyebrows as I studied him. Was he embarrassed?

"Jackson doesn't know." His voice was quiet like he'd just been caught with his hand in the cookie jar.

I wanted to ask why he cared, but I didn't want to hear the answer. Instead, I was going to move on. "So, you had me followed, and you showed up to my house with no reason. You accuse me of playing games, but you seem to be the only one moving pieces on the board." I forced my face to remain stoic even though my words sounded crazy.

Colten studied me. I felt as if I were melting under his gaze. I hated that he could read me like this. Like he knew exactly what I was thinking.

Having enough of this, I took a step forward only to realize that my leg had fallen asleep. My entire body weakened as I felt myself crashing to the floor. I braced myself for impact, but it never came.

Instead, I felt Colten's arms wrap around me, and suddenly, I was airborne. He pulled me to his chest as he stared down at me. I could see both concern and anger in his gaze.

"You okay?" he asked as his gaze raked over me.

I swallowed and slowly nodded. "Yeah. Just lost my balance."

Colten didn't answer. Instead, he brought me into the living room and set me down on the couch. He stood, studying my body. I felt exposed when he didn't let up.

"Do you have X-ray eyes?" I asked as I slowly brought my legs up to my chest and hugged my knees. Pressure started to build in my stomach, so I slowly pulled my legs away.

Colten looked confused. "What?"

"Nothing." I shrugged. "It just looks as if you are attempting to see through my jeans." And then I winced.

"I mean, assess my leg by just looking." My cheeks were on fire now. I needed to stop talking.

"Well, you have a tendency to hide things you should be telling people." His gaze met mine, and I could see that he knew.

He knew about the baby.

"Who told you?"

He shrugged as he sat down on the chair across from the couch. "Does it matter?" Then he paused. "You should have told me," he whispered.

My heart began to pound. I hated that he looked so hurt. Like I'd betrayed him. "I'm sorry. I wasn't ready to face it. Especially with Walker gone and the accident." I shrugged, hating that I'd lied to so many people who I cared about.

I didn't want to hurt anyone, yet it seemed like that was all I did.

"What did Walker say?" His voice was quiet, and I could tell that he hadn't wanted to speak the words.

"He doesn't know." The words were out before I had time to take stock of them. Why had I said that? Why didn't I just lie? Colten wasn't going to know the difference. He was here for a check-in and then would be leaving.

"You haven't told him?"

I shook my head. I knew I should have, and I really didn't have an excuse for why I'd kept it a secret this long. But I'd waited, and eventually it got easier to wait.

Plus, I wanted to make sure things were okay between us before I added another human into our mix.

"Is that why you came here? To make me feel bad about not telling Walker?" Tears were forming in my eyes. It was hard to rebuild a relationship that had felt so broken just a month ago. I didn't need Colten here making me feel like I was failing.

I already felt that way.

He didn't speak. Instead, he just sat there, studying me. Then he sighed and leaned back. "I'm sorry, Naomi. I know you're going through some things. I don't want you to think that I'm here just to throw shade." He gave me a soft smile. "I was worried about you, and your brother is being a punk."

I scoffed as I turned away to wipe the tears that had slipped loose. "You can say that again." I startled when I turned back around. Colten had stood up from his seat and was now inches away from me.

He leaned forward and grabbed a tissue from the end table. He handed it over, and I gratefully took it from him. "Thanks," I muttered.

His smile reemerged. "Well, I'm here. Might as well put me to work." He rolled his shoulders and looked around. "What can I do?"

3

PENNY

The drive to Harmony Island took longer than I'd anticipated. We stopped for meals and to fill up on gas, but that was about it. I was bone-dead tired when we pulled up to the Apple Blossom Bed and Breakfast on the island.

When I stepped out of the car, I could hear the crash of the waves and smell the salty water. The breeze washed over me, warming me and giving me chills at the same time. It was a strange sensation and made me smile.

Spencer shut the driver's door and moved to the trunk to pull out our suitcases. I met him there and grabbed hold of my suitcase. His body tensed. I could tell that he was stressed.

I glanced up and gave him a small smile. "You're doing great," I said.

Spencer met my gaze for a moment before dropping it and returning my smile. "I hope so."

We walked, hand in hand, to the front door. Soft yellow light glowed from inside and lit up the first-floor windows. The wraparound deck was full of rocking chairs and benches. Pumpkins and cornstalks decorated the front steps and the door. It made me smile.

I loved this time of year. It felt like the perfect backdrop to Spencer and his family reconnecting.

Spencer knocked, and we waited until the door opened. A woman who looked to be in her eighties appeared. Her pure white hair was pulled up into a messy bun with whisps of hair framing her face. She had on rainbow-speckled glasses, and her bright blue eyes sparkled when she saw us. "Spencer?" she asked as her gaze scanned over Spencer and then moved to me.

"Yes," he said, reaching out his hand.

They shook, and then Spencer nodded toward me. "This is Penny."

The woman turned to me. "Welcome. My name is Missy, and I own Apple Blossom."

"Nice to meet you, Missy," I said as we shook hands.

"Well, let's get you two inside. I just finished making some apple pie and some sweet tea." She pushed the door open further and then stepped back so we could enter.

"Leave your suitcases here. Harold will bring them up to your room."

Spencer looked as if he didn't like this idea, but

Missy gave him a look that said she would brook no argument, so he left it in the corner next to mine. She led us through the living room, which opened up to the dining room. There was a long, dark wood table in the center of the room. The decorations continued in here. The smell of cinnamon and nutmeg filled the ar.

A steaming pie sat on the buffet that spanned the far wall. A large pitcher filled with amber-colored tea and surrounded by glass cups sat next to it. Missy waved for us to take a seat and moved over to the food. Soon the sound of a knife hitting the sides of the ceramic pie plate filled the air.

I glanced over at Spencer, anxious to know how he was feeling about all of this. I was having a hard time reading him. He looked uncomfortable but was clearly trying to hide it from Missy, so he just looked as if he were in pain. I knew he wanted to get to bed so he could prepare himself for tomorrow, but Missy was keeping him from that.

My heart went out to the man. I reached over and wrapped my hand around his, squeezing gently, which turned his attention to me. I gave him a soft smile. "It'll be great," I whispered, hoping he knew that I was here for him no matter what.

I was going to help him through this.

He cleared his throat and nodded, but before he could speak, Missy turned to face us. She was grinning as she held two plates with giant pieces of pie plopped in the middle.

"You two are going to love my apple pie." She set the plates down in front of us. "I just picked the apples this morning." She leaned in. "They don't call this place Apple Blossom just because it sounds pretty." She gave us a wink and then leaned back, laughing.

I kind of adored Missy. She was sweet and sassy, and she cracked herself up. She wasn't a person who took herself too seriously, and it was refreshing. Having had the history I did—being stuck in a world where I constantly worried what others thought of me—the idea that I could be my own person was liberating.

"That's amazing," I said as I picked up my fork and took a bite. The crisp taste of the apples mixed with the buttery crust and was topped off with the cinnamon from the filling. It had my mouth dancing with pleasure.

I raised my eyebrows as I turned to Missy. She grinned and looked satisfied as she settled down on the chair across from us. It seemed she'd experienced this reaction before and knew exactly what it meant.

"I told you. I'm an award-winning pie maker." She threaded her fingers together and then rested her hands on the table in front of her. "Now, why don't you two tell me why you are here." She focused her attention on Spencer.

I could feel his entire body tense. Whatever relaxed feelings he got from eating the pie had fled, and he was back to stressing. That frustrated me, but Missy didn't seem like the kind of person who just let people keep to themselves. I had a feeling that she was the kind of woman who liked to be involved—with the purest of intentions.

"We're just visiting," I said, hoping that she would take her focus off Spencer and put it on me.

"Oh, I got that," she said as she flicked her gaze in my direction. "Most people who stay here are visiting." Then she narrowed her eyes. "Whom are we visiting? Can I help you locate them?" She leaned back in her chair and drummed her fingers on the table. "I've lived here my whole life. There isn't a person here on Harmony that I don't know."

I had no doubt that what she was saying was true, and it might be useful to have a local help us with sussing out Abigail and Sabrina. But Spencer had turned into a statue; he was clearly not interested in telling this stranger his life story.

"I think we're going to keep that to ourselves," I responded, hoping that she wouldn't get offended. After all, she had to be used to people not answering her questions.

"Ah, woman. Leave these two people alone. They don't need you poking around in their private life."

Surprised by the voice, I turned to see Harold standing in the doorway. He had a mug of what I assumed was coffee and a loving scowl on his face.

"Harold," Missy hissed as she turned to glare at him.

Harold just shrugged. "You're going to scare off all of our guests if you demand to know their deepest secrets."

"I'm not demanding to know anything. I am a fountain of knowledge. I'm just offering my services." She gave us a wide smile.

I could tell she was genuine, but that didn't change the fact that this story wasn't mine to tell. "We appreciate you offering, but we'd rather keep it close to our hearts." I gave her a soft smile. "You really have a beautiful home, and this pie is to die for."

I could sense Missy starting to soften as a smile tugged at her lips.

"It won first place last year at the Harmony fair."

I nodded. "I bet it did." Then I yawned. Spencer still hadn't spoken, so I glanced over at him and patted his hand. "Ready to head to bed?" I turned back to Missy. "We had a long drive and need to hit the hay."

Spencer was out of his chair before I could finish. He cleared his throat and nodded at Missy and Harold. "Thanks for your warm welcome, but it's time for us to go to bed." Missy moved to stand, but Spencer waved her away. "I think we can find the room."

"Oh, okay." She motioned toward the stairs. "First door at the top. The Cortland room."

I gave her a smile to tell her I appreciated that she'd named the rooms after different types of apples and then followed after Spencer, who was already making his way out of the dining room. I hurried to match his stride as he headed up the stairs.

Once we were in the room, he shut the door and growled.

"Staying here was a mistake," he said as he huffed and headed over to his suitcase.

"She was just trying to be nice." I settled down on the bed and started to remove my shoes.

Spencer didn't seem to hear me. He was throwing his clothes around as if he were looking for something. "Why did she want to know?" He growled again as if the memory was coming back to him. "The last thing we need is her poking around and spooking Abigail and Sabrina."

I stopped and looked over at him. "You didn't tell them we were coming?"

He glanced up at me. "No."

It was my turn to scoff. "What if they aren't even here?" My mind was whirling. "I gave you their numbers. You should at least have let them know we were coming."

Spencer fisted his pajamas and straightened. "Well, I didn't." And then he headed into the bathroom and shut the door.

I flopped back on the bed and sighed. This wasn't going how I'd pictured it. Which I should have known. With Spencer, nothing was exactly easy. I knew he meant well. He was just trying to process his history and figure out how he was going to have a future with his daughters.

When Spencer got out of the bathroom, he headed

straight to the bed and got under the covers. I rolled myself off the bed and headed over to my suitcase. I located my pajamas and toiletries and headed to the bathroom.

By the time I got out, Spencer was snoring. I pulled the covers off my side of the bed and climbed in. After applying lotion to my hands and arms, I flipped off my light and snuggled down under the comforter.

My stomach was in knots as I thought about Spencer's reaction to Missy. Sure, she was a nosy stranger who wanted him to talk about things he wasn't ready to deal with, but it worried me.

If this was how he was going to be the first hour we were here, how was he going to react when we actually confronted his daughters? When they expressed their feelings to him?

Was he ready for this?

My heart ached for this man. I wished that I could take away this pain. That I could somehow make everything okay. But I knew I couldn't do that. I needed to let him find peace on his own. It was the only way it would mean something to him.

He needed to take this journey, and I was here to support him.

One thing was for sure; I wasn't going anywhere.

I was here to stay.

4

NAOMI

It was probably naive of me to think that Colten would leave. He didn't bat an eye when I asked him to clean the bathroom or fold the towels. When I plopped down on the couch and proceeded to watch soap operas, he joined me. In fact, he got more invested in the show than I was, leaning forward on his elbows and staring at the screen.

He even shouted at the characters like he was yelling at a ref while watching a football game—like I'd seen him do so many times with Jackson.

I must have been staring because Colten's gaze was suddenly on me. He raised an eyebrow.

"You okay?" he asked.

Startled that I'd been caught, I blinked and turned my attention back to the screen. This wasn't how I'd planned this day to go. Even though I enjoyed having someone here with me, I couldn't help but feel like I was somehow cheating on Walker.

That thought made my cheeks heat. Maybe cheating was the wrong word. Disloyal was probably a better one. After all, he'd made it very clear how he felt about my brother and Colten when we left Magnolia. He didn't want me to have anything to do with my family.

Ever.

But here I was, blatantly disregarding his wishes. I knew I shouldn't let Colten in, but I did. The guilt was eating me alive—even if I so desperately wanted a friend right now.

"How long are you planning on staying here?" I asked as I unfolded my legs and stretched them out in front of me.

He leaned forward and grabbed a handful of popcorn from the bowl that was sitting on the coffee table. I'd made it earlier, but my stomach was too knotted to eat anything. "Trying to get rid of me already?" he asked, peering over at me.

I wanted to say no, but he'd always been good at reading me. He'd know I was lying before I even said it.

"Kind of," I whispered, hating that I even had to say this. I was mad at Walker for drawing a line in the sand, and I was even madder at my brother and Colten for pushing Walker away. If they'd only decided not to be jerks, I still might be able to have a relationship with all of them. We could be the family I so desperately wanted.

Colten seemed surprised at my answer. He raised his eyebrows as he leaned back on the couch. "Brutal honesty?" he asked before he shoved the popcorn into his mouth.

I sighed and shifted, trying to find a comfortable spot. I wanted to blame the lumpy couch that Walker and I had found at a consignment store, but I knew the real reason I was uncomfortable. I was angry with all of the men in my life.

"Colten, I'm just..." My voice faded as my words left me. I wasn't sure what I wanted to say. Everything seemed to fall flat around me. I was tired of it all, and I just wanted to get to a place of peace. It didn't feel like that was too much to ask, but it was starting to seem that way.

"I'm worried about you," he said, his voice taking on a deeper tone. One that I didn't recognize.

It made my emotions catch in my throat. "Why?"

He shrugged. "You're pregnant. You were in an accident. Walker's left you here alone." His gaze intensified as he met my own. "I care about you. A lot." His last two words deepened his voice.

I could feel his emotions not only in what he was saying, but by the way he was looking at me.

He meant it.

Tears formed in my eyes once again. Darn this pregnancy. I was ready for it to be over just so I could keep my composure.

"I care about you too," I whispered.

Colten furrowed his brow. "Then why do you keep trying to kick me out?"

I pulled my knees up to my chest and hugged them. The pressure in my stomach grew to the point of uncomfortableness, so I loosened my arms. Everything was changing, and it was hard to accept any of it.

"I don't want to inconvenience you. After all, you have a life and a job in Magnolia. Why would you want to spend this time with me?" I allowed myself to be vulnerable and looked over at him. I locked my gaze with his, and my heart began to pound. Why was he here, and why did he care so much?

He swallowed, the muscles in his jaw clenching as he did. He studied me, and for a moment, he looked as if he wanted to say something. For a moment, I wanted to know what that was. But then fear gripped my chest.

"I know you feel a loyalty to my brother, but I'll be okay. I'm fine." My voice was flat, making it sound like I was anything but fine, but I finished my sentence with a smile, hoping that it would deter him from learning the truth.

He sighed and shrugged. "I have the week off. I'm here, so I might as well help you get settled and keep you company." He met my gaze again. "Are you okay with that?"

No. But I wasn't going to say that. I feared what his looks meant. What the depth in his gaze was going to do to me over and over again. When he wasn't around, I could ignore it. But now, I was beginning to wonder if he wanted something more.

Idiot.

This was not how I moved on with my life. Entertaining a teenage crush was dumb. Sure, I'd always found Colten attractive—any woman with eyes would—but that needed to be in the past. I was with Walker now, and even though he and I hadn't broached the conversation of marriage since getting back together, I was carrying his child. I was meant to be with him.

"Do I have a choice?" I asked with a sigh.

Colten paused. "Of course."

I started. That was not what I was expecting. I glanced over at him to see that his gaze had intensified. He didn't break our contact.

He leaned in. "You always have a choice, Naomi."

I swallowed. The muscles in my neck prickled from the emotions that had lodged themselves there. I blinked a few times, the desire to cry once more overtaking me. I hated that I was a mess. And I hated that Colten was seeing me this way.

"Okay," I whispered.

He frowned. "Okay, you're going to choose? Or, okay, I can stay?"

I moved to stand. "Okay, you can stay."

He was on his feet in a matter of seconds. He was so fast, that I hadn't realized he was now only inches away from me. My whole body responded to his sudden appearance, and I found myself stepping back out of instinct.

If Colten noticed, he didn't say anything. Instead, he declared that he was headed to his car to collect his duffle bag. He did pause when he got to the front door and looked over his shoulder. "You're not going to lock me out once I leave, are you?"

I contemplated that for a moment and then shrugged. "Would it stop you from coming in?" I let my voice take on a teasing tone. It had been way too serious in this room for too long. We needed some fresh air.

Colten contemplated that for a moment before he shook his head. "Nope."

The door was shut before I could respond. With Colten temporarily gone, I stretched, pressing my hands to my lower back and curving my spine to relieve the stress that had built up there.

This was going to be an interesting week. My thoughts wandered to what Walker might think about Colten staying here, but then I pushed it out. Why would he care? After all, he was leaving for the better part of a month. I was alone. Why would it be a problem for me to have an old friend stay and help?

Just as I thought those words, an idea wormed its way into my mind. An idea that I'd been trying to ignore ever since my time in Magnolia. Something had changed with Colten—that was for sure. Something inside of me. I reacted when he was around. I reacted when he looked at me.

I was scared of what it meant. Scared of what Colten meant to me.

I shook my head and focused on tidying up the living room. This was a one-bedroom apartment, and there was no way I could have Colten sleep in the same room as me. If he was going to stay, it would have to be on the couch.

I put the fitted sheet on the cushions, and I was in the process of spreading out a blanket when Colten opened the door. He smiled when he saw me and used his foot to kick the door shut behind him. He raised his duffle bag as if to show me that his mission had been successful.

I nodded. "You'll be sleeping here," I said as I extended my hand toward the couch.

Colten nodded. "Perfect." He dropped his bag down next to the couch and glanced over at me. "What's the plan for the rest of the day? We cleaned and watched TV. What's next?"

I sighed. The last thing I wanted was to be his tour guide. I was tired, and the draw to get takeout and curl up in bed to eat was strong. But I didn't want to look like that much of a bum to Colten, so I shrugged.

"I was going to start looking for a job. Wanna explore Harmony Island with me?"

Colten furrowed his brow. "A job?"

"I can't sit around the house by myself all day," I hurried to add. The last thing I needed was a lecture about working while pregnant. I was a capable woman. I didn't need Colten looking out for me like that.

He studied me and then shrugged. "Sounds good." He glanced around the apartment. "So should we head out?"

I sighed, not really wanting him to come with me. But I knew that I wasn't going to be able to stop him. I clapped my hands and nodded. "Yep."

I changed into something more presentable, and we were out the door ten minutes later. The sun was high in the sky. The smell of salt water filled the air. It was still warm here in North Carolina, but every so often, a cool breeze flowed around us, reminding me that fall was just around the corner.

My apartment building was situated on the outskirts of town. Harmony Island was small and homey. A place where everyone knew everyone. When Walker and I had first gone into Godwins, the local grocery store, so many people greeted us. We were new, and no one knew who we were, yet they were excited to get to know us.

I was slowly learning people's names, but with the pregnancy fog, I was quick to forget.

"Wanna start here?" Colten asked as we neared the front doors of Godwins.

I glanced inside to see the familiar face of the woman who'd greeted us every time we'd gone in. I just couldn't remember her name. "Um..."

Colten raised his eyebrows, and then he sighed. "It's

probably best if we get as many applications as we can, so you have some to choose from."

He went inside before I could stop him. Of course, the woman who owned the store approached him. They shook hands, and I couldn't tell what they were saying until they both looked my direction and Colten made it even more evident that he was talking about me when he waved his hand in my direction.

Heat pricked my skin when the woman nodded and said something that looked like, *I know who she is.* They both waved me in, and I ducked my head and obeyed. When I stepped up next to Colten, he nudged me with his shoulder.

"Betty was telling me that she's looking for another cashier," Colten said.

Betty, that's right. I made a mental note to remember her name.

"Why didn't you tell me you needed a job, honey? I would have hired you weeks ago." Betty reached out and wrapped her arm around my shoulders.

I gave her a small smile. "We were getting settled."

She gave my shoulders a squeeze. "Why don't you go ask Maisy to get you an application?" Then she leaned forward. "She's my goddaughter, Lord bless her soul." Betty waved her hand in the direction of the blonde woman standing next to the open register. She was helping an older woman.

I nodded and hurried over to Maisy to get an application. I was ready to get out of the store. Colten and Betty picked up their conversation as soon as I was gone. Blast Colten. He had a way of finding friends everywhere.

I waited until Maisy handed the older woman her receipt and then leaned forward. "Betty said you could get me an application?" I asked.

Maisy glanced over at me. Her dark blue eyes were a stark contrast to her pale skin. Which was strange. Most people here were tanned and leathery. Not Maisy. Her skin looked like it was made of porcelain.

Realizing that I'd been staring a bit longer than was normal, I gave her a smile. She looked at me like I was weird and moved to open a drawer next to her. She ripped off one of the papers on the pad that she'd fished out and handed it over. "Here you go," she said just as another shopper approached her register.

I thanked her and then hurried over to Colten, who was still talking to Betty. I grabbed his hand and pulled him out of the store, effectively breaking off their conversation. Once we were outside, I kept walking.

"Naomi?" Colten asked. Suddenly, his hand was in mine, and he gave it a light squeeze.

I stopped walking and dropped my gaze down to our hands. Regret flushed through me, and I quickly dropped his hand. "I'm sorry," I mumbled. Heat was pricking at my skin as I peeked around us to make sure no one had caught us holding hands. The last thing I needed was for the small town to talk and for Walker to find out.

It had been innocent, but that never stopped the gossip train.

Colten shook his head. "It's fine. I'm just worried about you." He dipped down so that our gazes could meet. "Are you okay?"

Why did he keep asking this? I'd already told him. Not wanting him to see how exasperated I felt, I forced a smile and nodded. "Yes." When he looked like he didn't believe me, I sighed. "I just wanted to get out of there."

Colten looked confused, but he didn't ask me any more questions. Instead, he just nodded and led me down Main Street. We entered every shop we found. Colten kept his conversations short, only asking if they were hiring and for an application. It was as if he knew what I needed without me asking.

So much of this town was new to me, and I was still coping with the uncertainty of my future. With every place we stopped, my irritation toward Colten, and my life in general, began to lessen. Having Colten enter my life and take over...it was refreshing. It was what I needed in that moment, and it was bringing me so much relief.

The last stop was a small bookstore, *The Shop at the Corner.* It was adorable. As soon as we entered, a feeling of peace settled around me. There were bookcases lining every wall and a few jutting out in the middle, creating a maze. The smell of cinnamon and coffee had me breathing in deep.

I moved over to the books on one of the shelves and

ran my fingers over the spines. I'd always loved reading. When I was a child, I dreamed of being a famous writer and living in a big mansion in the woods where I would write and daydream.

Working here would be a dream come true.

"Can I help you two?" A woman with dark brown hair pulled up into a ponytail and dark brown eyes that hid behind a pair of navy-blue glasses appeared from around the bookshelf I was standing in front of.

I'd seen her around Harmony Island, but I hadn't introduced myself yet.

"Is this your store?" Colten asked as he approached us.

She nodded. "My name is Abigail." She glanced between us. "You two must be new here."

I nodded. "My name is Naomi."

"Naomi..." she said softly as if she were accessing a memory. Then she nodded. "You're the new couple that moved into Robbie's apartments."

"Yes," I said softly. It was still strange for so many people to know intimate details about my life.

"So, you're...Walker?" Abigail said as she turned her attention to Colten.

He parted his lips to speak, but I feared what he would tell her, so I stepped in.

"Yep," I said as I linked arms with him. "This is Walker."

My voice must have taken on a panicked tone because

Abigail looked startled. I could feel Colten tense next to me. From the corner of my eye, I saw his jaw tighten, but he didn't refute what I'd said. Instead, he just stood there, fuming.

"Well, I'm happy that you two have found me. Is there a particular book that you are looking for?"

I shook my head. "I'm actually looking for a job." My voice softened as fear grew inside of me and gripped my heart. Putting myself out there wasn't the easiest thing for me, and for some reason, the thought of working here seemed exciting. It would hurt for her to reject me.

"A job?"

I nodded.

She grew quiet as she glanced around. Then she nodded. "I guess we could use some help. My sister is pregnant, and I know she's going to need time off if it ends up being anything like the last one." Then her smile broadened. "What do you say?"

My ears were ringing. *Sister. Pregnant. Time off.* I wanted so badly to say yes, but what if the same thing happened to me? I didn't want to disappoint her.

"We'll take an application," Colten said.

His sudden words startled me. I turned to see him staring at Abigail, who'd smiled and headed toward the register. After pulling an application from a drawer, she handed it over.

We said goodbye, and she did the same. Once we were out on the street, I took a deep breath, but not before

Colten pulled his arm free from mine and rounded the nearest corner.

I hurried after him, worried about what he thought of me. Hoping I hadn't disappointed him too much. When I finally caught up with him, he was leaning on the side of the building with his arms folded. His gaze was focused on the ground, and I could tell that he was chewing on his thoughts.

"I'm sorry," I whispered as soon as I approached him.

Colten shook his head but didn't say anything.

"I shouldn't have told her that you were Walker. I was just..." I sighed as I pinched the bridge of my nose. I wasn't sure why I'd done that. "I guess I didn't want to have to get into my whole history and explain who you are and where Walker is." I met his gaze. "But I shouldn't have lied."

Colten's gaze was on me now. He stared at me, unrelenting. It made my heart hammer in my chest. What was he thinking? I couldn't tell what was behind his gaze. For some reason, all I could think was that I'd somehow hurt him—which would be strange. After all, we were old friends. So, what if I wanted him to play along with a little white lie?

Finally, he sighed and pushed himself off the wall. I waited for his response, but it never came. He shrugged and shoved his hands into his front pockets.

"Come on," he said as he nodded toward the road, "I'm starving."

5

PENNY

I woke the next morning feeling more optimistic about Spencer, his daughters, and our plan to reunite them. The sun was streaming through the open window, and I stretched out on the bed before allowing my body to sink back into the mattress. Missy certainly knew how to pick mattresses, that was for sure.

After my stretch, I kept my hand extended as I felt around the bed. When I came up empty-handed, I pushed myself up and glanced around the room. Sure enough, I was alone.

"Spencer?" I called out, tipping my ear toward the bathroom to see if that's where he'd snuck off to. But I didn't hear water running.

I didn't want to get out of bed. But, wondering where Spencer was, I pulled off the covers and slipped my feet to the floor. I padded across the room and stopped at the bathroom, knocking a few times.

Nothing.

Huh. I was alone.

I glanced around the room, hoping to see a note of some kind, but I didn't find anything. Worried that he'd gotten cold feet and left for Magnolia, I changed out of my pajamas into a white blouse and jeans. I threw my hair up into a ponytail and left the room with a bare face.

I headed down the stairs, panic settling in my gut, until I heard Spencer's familiar voice. All of a sudden, my adrenaline came crashing down, and my body went numb. I was angry and relieved at the same time.

I must have looked crazed, because as soon as I entered the dining room, Spencer's eyebrows rose. He was sitting at the table with a steaming plate of eggs and bacon. Missy was standing next to the buffet. She was currently stocking the huge platter of muffins in front of her.

"You okay, darling? You look like you've seen a ghost."

I patted my cheeks before combing my fingers through my hair. I forced a smile and nodded. "I slept wonderfully. Except when I woke up, alone." I glared at Spencer, who had returned his attention to his plate of food and slipped a heaping pile of eggs into his mouth.

"Men. They'll always go where their stomachs lead them."

I snorted. "Apparently."

Spencer swallowed. "Hey, I was being nice. You were

sleeping so soundly that I didn't want to wake you up. I was being a gentleman."

I shook my head as I grabbed a plate. If only Missy weren't here, I'd have a lot more to say to him. Spencer had a tendency to shut me out when things got hard. The last thing I needed was another man leaving me without talking to me. I hadn't had a lot of relationships since Maggie's father, but I knew I didn't like the feeling of being left behind.

I decided it was best to leave those thoughts and focus on breakfast. After filling a plate with fresh fruit, eggs, and a freshly baked biscuit, I grabbed a fork and a mug of coffee and moved to sit down next to Spencer.

Missy stepped back to survey the buffet and then tsked like she'd forgotten something. Once she disappeared into the kitchen, I turned to focus on Spencer. "I thought you'd left for Magnolia."

Spencer's mouth was full of muffin. His gaze met mine, and I studied him. He quickly chewed and swallowed before reaching for his glass of milk.

"Why would you think that?"

I stared at him. Was he serious? Anything to do with Rosalie or his daughters had him shutting me out. I wasn't going to lie, it hurt. "Just from the way you were acting last night." I wanted to add, *"And the reality of what today would bring,"* but I decided to keep that to myself.

Spencer shook his head. "I made a promise to Rosalie that I was going to fix this. So that's what I'm going to do."

"You did?"

"What?"

My throat felt as if it were closing. "You made a promise to Rosalie?"

He studied me before nodding. "Yes."

"When?" How much was Spencer not telling me?

"The weekend I went away to fish, I stopped by her grave." He picked up his bacon and took a bite. "Why?"

I pushed the eggs around my plate, desperate for something to distract me. I knew I shouldn't feel hurt. After all, it was his late wife and his family, but I couldn't help but wonder why he'd kept it from me. It felt as if he were trying to live two different lives. As if he didn't want me to partake in his past like I'd allowed him to partake in mine.

Sure, he'd invited me to Harmony Island with him. And I originally thought that it meant things were becoming deeper between us. But I was starting to worry that was only a pipe dream. If felt like I was here for him to lean on but not participate.

That thought felt selfish. After all, he was the one who was struggling. But I couldn't help but wonder who I was to Spencer. And who I would never become.

My emotions lodged themselves in my throat. I tried to clear them, but nothing worked. So, I decided to focus on my food.

"No reason, just wondering," I said quickly between bites.

I could see Spencer study me from the corner of my eye. But I didn't allow that to distract me from eating. I needed something other than my emotions to focus on, and eating breakfast seemed like the perfect distraction.

Missy returned to the dining room with a plate of freshly cooked sausage. I wondered who she was making all of this food for since it seemed to be just Spencer and I staying here. But I really wasn't in the mood for small talk, so I kept my thoughts to myself.

It didn't take long for my question to be answered. A few minutes after she'd laid out the sausage, the front door of the bed and breakfast opened and two men in lime-green construction shirts appeared. They were laughing and talking as they walked in.

"Hey, Ma," the tall one with blond hair said as he approached Missy and gave her a kiss on her cheek.

"Mrs. Hodges," the other one said as he removed his ball cap and gave her a wide smile.

"Oh, William, I told you to call me Missy."

William shook his head. "No, ma'am. My mom would have a fit if she knew that." He replaced his cap. "I value my life."

Missy waved him away and turned to her son. "I hope you're hungry," she said with a smile.

He nodded. "Starved." And then as if he suddenly realized Spencer and I were sitting at the table, he leaned forward. "I'm sorry. We didn't know there were going to be guests here."

Missy clapped her hands. "That's my fault. Where are my manners?" She turned to smile at us and then waved toward her son. "This is Jack, my son. Jack, this is Penny and Spencer. They are visiting the island."

Jack nodded. "Nice to meet you."

"Jack and William come by every morning on their way to work for some food." Missy swatted Jack's arm. "If I didn't feed them, they'd be skin and bones." She was trying to pretend as if she were annoyed, but I could tell she loved it. I didn't blame her. I loved it when Maggie needed me. Even though she was grown.

Taking care of people seemed to be Missy's specialty, and her son and his friend were no exception. She ushered them to their seats and then busied herself with filling up their plates. When she set them down in front of Jack and William, their eyes widened.

"Geez, Ma! We're going to have a hard time fitting into our pants if you keep feeding us this way." Jack patted his stomach, which only made me snicker.

There was no way there was anything but a six-pack under his shirt. I looked over at Spencer, and he seemed to be thinking the same thing—to be young again.

"So, are you visiting family?" William asked after about half his plate was cleaned.

I glanced over at him and then back to Spencer. "We're..." I wasn't sure how to say this. I didn't want to overstep, but I also didn't want William to think that we were ignoring him. Or for Missy to think that there was more to our story and start pestering us.

She seemed like a nosy but sweet neighbor to those who stayed at the Apple Blossom B&B.

"We're..." Spencer seemed as stumped as I was on how to answer that question. Just when I thought both boys would think that Spencer and I were having a brain malfunction, Spencer quickly continued, "We're just visiting. Harmony Island seemed like a perfect place to come and recharge."

"Oh, it is," Missy said as she sat down at the head of the table. Her plate was full of fruit, and she speared a piece of watermelon. "You guys came at the perfect time. The Thanksgiving festival is this weekend, and you are going to die when you see this town decked out in all its decorations." She shivered from excitement. "It's like a movie."

"You may be overselling it a bit, Ma," Jack said as he raised his hand in our direction.

"Jackson Mortenson Hodges, I am not." She turned her focus on us. "Don't let my stick-in-the-mud son make you think anything less. It's a paradise for the holiday enthusiast." Then her voice softened. "Do you guys appreciate the finer art of holiday decorations?"

Her words made me think of the harvest festival Magnolia held. It was perfect in every sense of the word, so I understood her frustration when her son wanted to paint it as something less.

"Our hometown has something similar." I nodded to Missy. "And it is spectacular."

Missy looked content as she nodded her head in Jack's direction. Even though they weren't in an argument, I could tell that she felt supported.

"What?" Jack asked with a smile on his lips. "I didn't say it was bad. I just said you might be overselling it a bit."

Missy waggled her finger in his direction. "I'm selling it perfectly."

Jack shrugged and began stabbing his eggs.

"So, when does this festival take place?" I asked. I wasn't sure how things were going to go with Spencer, so having something to do while he figured it out was just what I needed.

"It starts tomorrow and goes through the week. We have festivities every night, with the barn dance on Saturday rounding out the festival." She grew quiet as she eyed me. "Why? Are you looking to volunteer?"

Jack's gaze flicked to me, and I could tell that he was trying to tell me to walk away, but I just smiled. I'd dealt with the pickiest publishers in the publishing world. I could handle his mother.

"If you need some help."

Missy clapped her hands as she moved to stand. "Wonderful! I lost some of my regulars this year and was worried I was going to have to carry this load myself." She hurried over to the kitchen only to return with a clipboard, which she handed over.

When I saw the list, I wondered what I'd gotten myself into, but Missy didn't look like she was going to accept my resignation. I was helping her if I wanted to or not.

"Tonight is our final meeting, so make sure you come." She paused as she glanced around. "Will that be a problem?"

I glanced over at Spencer who shook his head. My stomach sank from his reaction. He didn't want me around —which I was trying to accept—but it was hard. I wanted him to need me, but I doubted he did.

"It should be fine," I said as I tucked the clipboard under my arm. Spencer had finished his breakfast, and there was no way I was going to let him scoot upstairs and leave me down here with Missy.

He was going to talk to me whether he wanted to or not.

I thanked Missy for the food and said goodbye to Jack and William. They waved to me as I hurried through up the stairs, where I found Spencer unlocking the door to our room.

Once inside, I shut the door behind me and turned to face him. He was standing in front of the bathroom mirror, staring at his reflection as if he were deep in thought.

"Is everything okay?" I asked. I kept close to the wall perpendicular to the door. For some reason, I feared that if I got too close, I would spook him, and he'd run further away from me than he already was.

He glanced over at me. "Why?"

I swallowed. I could feel him pulling away, and I hated it. I couldn't help but wonder if I'd done something wrong. "You're quiet."

He sighed as he turned on the faucet and held his hands underneath it. He let them fill up before splashing the water over his face. "I'm just struggling, Penny." He splashed his face a few more times before reaching for a towel.

I wanted to scream. I wanted to shake him. I hated how he was leaving me completely in the dark. Why wouldn't he just open up to me? He visited Rosalie's grave without telling me. He left the room this morning without telling me.

What else wasn't he telling me?

Here I was, thinking that we'd grown closer, when in fact it had been the exact opposite. He was determined to keep me at arm's length.

How long was it going to be like this? It wasn't like I was a spring chicken or anything. If I had to spend the majority of my life trying to decipher his meanings, then I was in trouble. I wanted a fulfilled life, and I wanted it with Spencer.

But that didn't seem possible at this moment.

"Anything I can do to help?" I asked, not really sure if he was going to answer, and not really sure what I was going to do if he did.

He sighed as he hung the towel back up. Then he turned to face me. "I'm worried."

"About your daughters?" I asked. My heart began to pound as my mind raced. Somewhere in my deepest, darkest thoughts, I wondered if he was worried about me.

About us.

Was reuniting with his daughters going to be a good or a bad thing for our relationship? Was he going to remember all that he'd had with Rosalie and leave me in the dust?

Was I a fool to keep pushing for him to reconnect with his daughters?

As much as I wanted to be selfish and keep Spencer all to myself, I knew that he was never going to feel complete until he reconciled with his family. I wanted that reconciliation to include me, but if it didn't, at least I would know that he was happy.

That was all I wanted for him.

Spencer took in a deep breath and planted his fists on the bathroom counter. He tipped his head down and remained silent for a few moments before glancing over at me. "I'm worried that I can't be the man you want me to be."

My expression fell. He must have seen it because he pushed off the counter and stood, folding his arms.

"It's not that I don't care about you." His voice took on a softer tone. I could hear his affection toward me, but I couldn't ignore what he was saying.

His words felt like knives to my gut.

"But..." I whispered, wishing that he would just get on with what he was saying. If he wanted me to leave, I'd rather he tell me now than later on when I was more invested in this town, his family...and him.

"But I'm not sure I can be what you want me to be. At least not right now." His expression was pained, and I knew that this was hard for him to say. I'd known that this whole relationship was going to be hard. As soon as I saw Rosalie's picture on the bathroom counter, I knew it was going to be a wound that Spencer would struggle with healing.

It hurt, hearing him say those words. I wanted him to take them back. I didn't want him to continue down this path. But he'd already started, and there was no way I could ask him to retreat. All I could do—the *right* thing to do—was to stand aside and let him do what he needed to.

"I understand," I said softly as I folded my arms. "I'm here if you need me, but don't feel like you have to include me in everything. It's not like we're—" My brain stopped my words. I was just about to say married. It was something we'd discussed in passing, but nothing to the extent of what our intentions were for this relationship in the long run.

It was strange, having a relationship at an older age. When I was younger, there was a push to get married to start a family. We were both too old for that now; if we wanted a relationship, it was solely for ourselves.

I knew I wanted Spencer for the long haul, however that would come about. But I wasn't sure he wanted the same.

Spencer glanced over at me as my unspoken words lingered in the air. I offered him a smile, hoping to convey that I didn't expect anything from him and that it had just been a slip of the tongue. It felt like an eternity before he nodded. He pushed his hand through his hair and then nodded toward the shower.

"I'm going to get cleaned up and then head out. I want to clear my head before I attempt to meet up with Abigail and Sabrina." He sighed. "Do you think you'll be okay without me?"

I released the breath I'd been holding through my lips, making a *pfft* sound. Heat pricked my cheeks when I realized that I must have looked like a dork. I settled on a simple nod. "I'll be perfect. Plus, Missy seems to have a lot for me to do. If I ask, I have no doubt that she'll put me to work right away."

Spencer paused as he met my gaze once more. "Okay."

I didn't get a chance to reply. He shut the bathroom door, and a few seconds later, I heard the water turn on.

Now alone, I collapsed on the bed, falling back onto the soft sheets. I closed my eyes for a moment, tears forming on my eyelids. I didn't want to cry. I didn't want to despair.

I didn't want to allow the thought that things might be over between us.

Even though I knew it might just be avoiding the inevitable, it didn't matter. I wasn't going to leave until Spencer said those words.

Until then, I would hope.

After all, that was all I had left.

6

NAOMI

I woke the next morning, stiff but surprisingly relaxed. I stretched out on my bed, allowing my arms to fall to my sides and my body to sink further into the mattress. It was strange. Dinner last night with Colten had thankfully been more relaxed than our rendezvous outside of the bookstore.

We'd talked about life and the past. There were even a few times I laughed. It was like the old days—minus Jackson.

And I...missed it.

I missed Colten. I missed my old life.

A flutter passed across my stomach, and my entire body froze. I'd had a baby app installed on my phone, and it said that I should start feeling fluttering any day now.

Could that have been the baby?

It happened again.

"Colten!" I yelled. I needed him to feel it too. I needed someone to tell me that I wasn't crazy. "Colten!" I yelled again.

Suddenly, my bedroom door swung open, and Colten stumbled into my room. His hair was tousled, and he looked as if he were struggling to wake up. "What's wrong?" he asked as he pushed his hand through his hair.

I was going to just ignore the fact that he looked incredible. He was wearing a white t-shirt that I could see his muscles through, and a pair of black basketball shorts. My heart picked up speed, but I instantly hushed it.

There wasn't time for that.

"Come here," I said, beckoning him to the bed. There was no way I was going to move, in case that changed the baby's willingness to kick.

Colten hesitated. He was finally waking up, and it seemed as if he wasn't sure he wanted to obey.

"I won't bite," I said as I raised my hand and waved him over.

He paused, but a moment later he shook his head as if he were dispelling a silly thought and walked over. Once he was standing over my bed, a flood of regret washed through me. What was I doing? Why was I asking him to get closer?

Another fluttering pushed aside all of those thoughts. I leaned forward to grab his hand and pulled him toward the bed. I must have yanked too hard because, suddenly, he was on top of me, bracing his body with both hands.

His face was inches from mine as he kept himself from crashing onto me.

"What are you doing?" he asked, the tone in his voice turning husky.

"I...uh..." I blinked, trying to process my thoughts. Colten was on my bed, above me, because I'd pulled him down on me.

Why did I pull him down on me?

Before I could decide how to respond, Colten pressed up on his hands and sat next to me on the bed. With him off of me, I suddenly felt like I could think. I shifted in the bed, attempting to bring my body away from his, and glanced over at him.

The reason I called him into the room came rushing back to me, and I extended my hand. Colten paused before meeting my gaze.

"What?" he asked.

Not wanting to make a big deal out of this, I wiggled my fingers. If there was nothing going on between us, I needed to act like it. "Give me your hand."

He raised his hand from the bed and held it in front of him. "This hand?" He flexed it a few times.

I nodded. "Yes."

He narrowed his eyes. "Why?"

I sighed. "Nothing bad, I just need to know something."

He glanced down at his hand. "You need to know something from my hand?"

Sighing, I reached out and grabbed a hold of it. Then I pulled off the covers and put his hand just over my belly.

He looked both startled and stunned. Forcing myself to believe that this meant absolutely nothing, I pulled up my pajama shirt, so my stomach was exposed and pressed his hand to my skin.

As soon as he touched me, I sucked in my breath. His hand was warm and covered most of my stomach. Not wanting him to see what his touch was doing to me, I pressed his fingers where I'd felt the baby move. "Do you feel that?"

When he didn't respond, I glanced over at him. Colten's gaze became cryptic as he studied me. Then, as if he suddenly realized that I was staring at him, he blinked. "Feel what?" he asked, his voice deep and husky.

"The baby."

He furrowed his brow as he turned his attention to my stomach. Then he stilled his body and leaned closer to me. "You felt the baby?" he asked, pressing into my stomach with the pads of his fingers.

My skin responded and goosebumps rose where he touched me.

"I think so." I breathed, unable to speak fully. I hadn't expected to feel this way from Colten's touch. The response left me breathless and confused. I wanted to push away, but I also wanted to...stay.

He paused as he tipped his head toward the bed. As if listening would help him focus. Then his gaze met mine and held it. I thought he was going to break it off after a few seconds, but he didn't. Instead, he remained staring at me.

There was something in his gaze. Something deep in the way he looked at me. It made my heart pound so hard I could hear it in my ears. It wasn't the kind of look you give a friend. And it wasn't the kind of look you give your best friend's little sister.

It was something more.

And my entire body was reacting.

"Can you feel it?" I asked. I needed this to be over. I needed to pull away. This was not supposed to be happening. He wasn't supposed to make me feel this way. Everything about this situation confused me.

If I loved Walker, why was it so easy for me to react to Colten? Why was he able to make me feel liked? Wanted? Desired?

I'd been around men long enough to know when they were interested. And Colten was interested.

Why?

I was pregnant. I was in a messy relationship. I was damaged and hurt. I'd hurt *him*. Why would he even want to entertain these thoughts?

As if he could read my mind, Colten dropped his gaze and pulled his hand away. He stood up and stepped back, away from me. A huge weight lifted off my chest the further he got from me.

I pulled my shirt down to cover my stomach, regretting

that I'd even asked him to come in. I grabbed a nearby pillow and hugged it to my chest. I took in a deep breath. "Sorry I woke you up. I was just excited, and I wanted to know if you could feel it too." I slowly brought my gaze up to meet his. "That's all."

He had his hands shoved into the front pockets of his shorts. His shoulders were rounded, and he nodded. "I get it. You were excited." He shrugged. "I'm sorry I couldn't feel it."

I waved away his words. "No worries. It was silly to think someone else could feel the baby when I wasn't even sure I was feeling it myself." I brought up my knees as far as I could and wrapped my arms around them. "It'll probably be a few more weeks before someone else can feel the kicks."

Just in time for Walker to get home.

Walker.

I squeezed my eyes tight. What was wrong with me? I had someone that I cared about. Someone that was going to come home and plan a life together with me. The father of the baby that was growing in my stomach.

The last thing I needed was to allow my schoolgirl crush to get in the way. It wasn't fair to Walker, and it certainly wasn't fair to Colten. I needed to get my head on straight and focus.

"I think I want to take a shower now," I said slowly, hoping that he would get the hint that I wanted him to leave.

A panicked look flashed across his face as he took a step back. "Oh, okay. I'm sorry," he mumbled before turning and hurrying out of my room.

With the door now shut, I slunk under my covers, pulling them over my head and burying my face in the fabric. There was something wrong with me. Something *very* wrong.

I was a glutton for punishment, that was for sure. I was entertaining feelings for a man I had no business entertaining feelings for.

If I were smart, I would tell him to leave right now. Sure, I'd be alone here in Harmony, but alone was better than confused. Alone was better than hurt.

With Colten gone, I could focus on the baby. Focus on finding a job. Focus on getting ready for when Walker got home.

That was the life I wanted. It was what I chose. I needed to remember that.

Feeling frustrated with myself and hoping that a shower would help wash away my confusion and guilt, I climbed out of bed and headed into the bathroom.

After a hot shower and a good scrub down, I wrapped a towel around my body and stepped out. I dried off and dressed in something simple. I wasn't trying to impress anyone. Colten was a nobody to me.

After running my brush though my hair and applying the simplest of makeup, I slipped my sandals on and headed out of my room. The smell of eggs and pancakes filled my nose as I shut my door behind me.

My mouth watered as I made my way to the kitchen. "What smells amazing?" I asked as I rounded the corner.

The sight in front of me caused me to stop. Colten's back was to me as he stood in front of the stove. For a moment, I racked my brain for the last time I saw Walker making me anything. His version of food was a box of cereal and a carton of milk. And even then, he rarely made that for me.

So having Colten standing there, making breakfast for me...was strange.

If my goal was to forget the feelings growing inside of me for Colten, this wasn't helping.

"I could have done that," I said as I walked into the kitchen.

Colten glanced over his shoulder before returning his attention to the stovetop. "I know you could have." Then he shrugged. "But I decided to do it." His smile made me angry, and when he accompanied it with a wink, heat pricked at my collar.

I don't know why my thoughts took on a snippy hint, but I was irritated. Irritated that he was here. Irritated that Walker didn't treat me this way. And irritated that the longer Colten stayed here, the harder it was going to be for me to see him go.

Even the thought caused my stomach to churn.

I was getting used to him, and I hated that.

I wanted to retort with something quippy, but I realized that anything I was going to say would sound stupid. So, I poured myself a large glass of water and headed over to the table. Colten was dishing up some food on two plates, and I was starving. I would think better once I had a full stomach.

And I was right.

Not only were the warm eggs and sweet pancakes exactly what I needed, but the silence between the two of us was calming. It was strange, sitting next to Colten and not feeling as if I needed to talk.

We were completely content to just be in each other's presence.

After my plate was clean, I set my fork down and leaned back in my chair, letting my stomach expand. The baby was beginning to take up room already. I couldn't imagine what it would be like when I was eight or nine months pregnant.

I must have had a strange look on my face because, when I turned around, Colten was studying me.

I frowned and then shrugged. "What?" I hated that he always looked like he was analyzing me. It left me feeling raw and bare. A sensation I hated.

I needed to be strong. I feared what would happen to me if I wasn't. I was so close to breaking, that one little nick to the wall I'd built up around me would see it all come tumbling down.

"I was just wondering what you were thinking about."

He shrugged as he leaned back in his chair as well. "You had a sort of content yet worried look on your face."

My cheeks heated. He'd pegged my emotions and thoughts perfectly. "I was thinking about the baby," I whispered.

His gaze flicked down to my stomach, and for a moment, I wondered if he'd blush. But then he smiled. "Yeah? What were you thinking?"

I wasn't sure if I should be honest with him. But he'd asked. "How an eight-pound baby could fit in here," I said as I circled around my stomach with my hand.

He paused as if my words had shocked him. I smiled, liking the fact that I'd managed to startle him into silence.

"Or how I'm going to push a baby out," I continued, enjoying the sort of power I felt from this conversation.

Colten's cheeks were bright red now. I didn't feel bad. After all, he'd confronted me about my issues with Walker and living here in Harmony; it was payback time.

"Um...yeah..." he said, clearing his throat. He reached forward and grabbed my plate and then pushed his chair back.

Not wanting to let him off the hook quite yet, I moved to follow him. "If I'm going to get an epidural. Or how long that needle is. What if I need an episiotomy?" Colten's face paled. Being a police officer, I knew he'd been trained in first aid. Assisting in births was a part of that. But just to make sure he understood, I continued, "That's when they cut you—"

Colten whipped around and pulled me to him. He placed his hand over my mouth, and the pleading in his gaze took my breath away. It didn't help that his hand was also pressed firmly into my lower back as he held me against him. My hands were sprawled out against his chest so I could brace myself. I could feel his heart pounding in his chest. It matched the cadence of my own.

"I don't know what you are doing, but you need to stop," Colten said. His voice was gruff, and there was a hint of desperation there. He held my gaze for a moment before he slowly dropped his hand. "I'm not scared of what you are going to go through. What you are saying doesn't worry me." He dropped his hand from around my waist and took a step back.

I suddenly felt chilly from the lack of his warmth. I folded my arms, wrapping my hands around my upper arms. He'd startled me into silence, and I was having a hard time finding my bearings well enough to respond.

Colten was leaning against the counter now. His hands were tucked into his front pockets, and his legs were extended out in front of him. His gaze was focused on the ground. His brows were knit together, and I could tell that he was analyzing what he was going to say next.

"Then what worries you?" I finally asked, startling myself. He'd left his train of thought open-ended, and I thought I was okay with it, but apparently not.

Colten looked up at me, his pained expression taking my breath away. He looked unsure, not because he didn't know the answer, but because he feared what I was going to say.

"Do you really want to know?" he asked, his tone deepening.

I chewed my bottom lip. I wanted to say no, I really did, but that would have been a lie. And the truth was, the answer to this question would eat me alive until I knew. So, I nodded. I feared how I would sound if I spoke.

He sighed and then glanced toward the cupboards. "I'm worried that I missed my chance."

I blinked, not expecting that response at all. I stared at him, wondering if I'd missed something. "What?" I asked, stepping closer to him.

Colten didn't look at me right away. Instead, he took his time meeting my gaze. He held it for a moment, and just when I thought he was going to explain, he shrugged. "Never mind."

The silence that fell around us was deafening. I studied him, wanting him to continue. To explain himself. Instead, he clapped his hands and pushed off the counter. The moment we had before was gone, and he was back to smiling the way that made me want to shake him.

Like we were back to being just friends.

He rubbed his hands together. "So, what's the plan for today?"

I parted my lips, but nothing came out. I felt whiplashed, and I wasn't sure what I would say.

Colten looked as if he'd moved on from our conversation, and I didn't want to keep harping on it.

For now, I was going to pretend that I didn't hear what I wasn't sure he'd even said. Instead, I was going to move forward with my life.

That was the only way I was going to survive any of this.

7

PENNY

Despite my conversation with Spencer that morning and the lack of response to any of my texts, I was enjoying myself. Harmony Island was beautiful. The warm ocean breeze washed over me as I walked down Main Street, and I took in a deep breath.

This place reminded me of a warmer, brighter version of Magnolia. All I needed was Maggie here with me, and it would feel like home.

I loved the small shops that lined the street. Whoever built them had an eye for architecture and color. They weren't your normal square buildings. They were each unique, not only in their design but in their coloring as well.

It was like stepping into a storybook.

And the smells that came from the restaurants had my mouth watering.

I was standing outside of a fudge shop when my phone rang. For a moment, I hoped it was Spencer calling to tell me he'd been wrong, and he wanted me to be a part of his life. But it was Maggie.

I didn't want to sound disappointed, but she must have sensed it when I answered, because she didn't even bother to say hi. Instead, she asked, "What's wrong?"

"Nothing's wrong," I said as I finally gave into my craving and pulled open the door to the fudge shop. The smell of sugar and chocolate activated my salivary glands, and my mouth began to water.

"You sound upset," Maggie said.

"I'm not upset. I'm about to buy half a pound of fudge. Would someone who's upset do something like that?" I winced when my own argument hit my ears. I sounded pathetic.

"That is exactly what someone who is upset would do." Maggie grew quiet for a moment. "Did something happen with Spencer?"

My emotions choked my throat as tears pricked my eyes. I knew I shouldn't lie to Maggie, but I didn't want her to worry. "No," I said softly.

Maggie tsked. I knew she wouldn't believe me, but it was worth a shot. "What did he do? Did he leave? Do I need to come down there?"

The woman behind the counter finished up with a customer and turned her sights on me. I pointed toward the rocky road fudge and mouthed, *"half a pound."* She nodded and got busy filling my order.

"You're so sweet, but you don't need to come down here. And Spencer didn't leave me. He's just going through some things. I understand, and I'm keeping my distance like he asked." I sighed. Saying the words was easier than doing it. But I was going to be the person that Spencer needed, however he needed me.

Maggie was quiet. Just when I wondered if I'd dropped her call, she spoke. "Mom, I love you, and I want to protect you."

The woman behind the counter finished filling my order and waved me over to the register.

"I know, Mags. But this is a process that Spencer has to go through, and I want to make sure that I'm here to help him. He needs me. So, I'm going to stay."

The woman motioned to the credit card reader, so I swiped my card.

"I get it, Mom." Maggie sighed. I could tell that she was stressed, and I was sure my issues weren't helping any. "But I worry about you. Promise you'll call me if it gets bad?"

My heart hurt for my daughter. I wished that I had been a better mom. I wasted so many years keeping my distance from her, and I would do anything to get them back. "I know, and I will."

The woman handed me my bag, and I mouthed a thank you. She responded with a smile and nod. I turned, waiting for Maggie to reply as I walked out of the store. There was no way I was going to hang up without knowing that she was going to be okay.

The warm morning air hit me once more as I stepped out onto the sidewalk. I took in a deep breath and sighed. "I'll be okay. And I promise I will let you know if I need anything. For now, stay at the inn and focus on something else." I tipped my face toward the sky and allowed the warm sunrays to hit my skin. I needed this. I could literally feel my mood lifting as I stood there.

"Promise?" Maggie asked.

I nodded. "Promise."

We said our goodbyes, and I pulled my phone down from my cheek but left it clutched in my hand as I dropped my arm to my side. I took in another deep breath. I was going to be okay. I was. Spencer would come around, and we would move forward in our relationship.

It wasn't like Spencer was the type to spook...except he was. My stomach dropped. He'd ended up in Magnolia for that exact reason. He'd gotten scared and ran.

Was I really so certain that he wouldn't do the same here?

But the response to that question never came into my mind. Suddenly I was rammed into. The force caused me to step forward, and thinking I was going to need to catch myself, I dropped both my bag of fudge and my phone. My eyes whipped open, and I saw a woman's wide, panicked eyes looking down at me.

"I'm so sorry," she said as she grabbed onto my arm to steady me. "I didn't see you there."

I glanced down at the book that was lying next to my phone and fudge. I should have been angry, but I couldn't when I saw that she was reading one of Jackson's books. The one that I'd personally helped him workshop a few years ago.

"It's fine," I said as I reached down to gather our spilled items.

"No. I should know better than to walk and read." She reached out her hand for her book.

I wasn't in a hurry. I flipped it over and read the back —even though I already knew what was written there. I could recite it word for word in my sleep. "Is it good?"

The woman breathed. "It's amazing. Every time I think I know who the murderer is, it changes. Jackson Richard has a way of painting a picture."

I nodded. I had those feelings as well. If he didn't have his medical issues, I would have pushed him to keep writing. But I knew that quitting was what he wanted, and with Fiona and Blake, I knew it was what he needed.

That didn't make his retirement any less of a shame.

"What part are you on?" I asked as I handed back the book.

She took it and nodded in gratitude. She was young— Maggie's age. Her dark brown hair was pulled back into a ponytail, and a pair of navy glasses sat perched on her nose. "The main character is about to walk into a dark alley." She leaned forward. "I think he's about to find another dead body."

My lips tipped up into a smile. I knew exactly where she was, but I didn't want to spoil it for her. "I can see why you were completely engrossed."

She nodded. "It's a blessing and a curse." She adjusted her glasses. "As a fellow bibliophile, if you are looking for a good read, you should stop by my shop later." She tucked her book in the crease of her arm so that she could dig around in her purse. She pulled out a business card and handed it over to me.

"The Shop Around the Corner Bookstore?" I read. "Isn't that from a movie?" I swore I'd heard it before.

She rolled her eyes. "Yes. But it was named before that movie came out." She leaned in. "I'm convinced they stole it from my grandmother."

I nodded. "Probably." I turned the card over. "You own the bookstore?"

She nodded. "My grandmother owned it before me. When she passed away, I came here to take it over." Then she shrugged. "Well, me and my sister."

I blinked as my body went cold. I studied her, suddenly seeing a familiar set of dark brown eyes. She didn't look much like Spencer, just in a few areas. "What's your name?" I held my breath, praying that she wasn't who I feared she was. I wasn't sure how Spencer would feel if I met up with his daughter before him.

"Abigail," she said as she extended her hand. "And yours?"

Not sure what to do, I decided to rely on etiquette and shook her hand. "Penelope, but you can call me Penny."

Abigail smiled as she dropped her hand. "It's nice to meet you, Penny." Then she tapped the business card that I was still holding. "Make sure to stop by. I love to talk books."

I nodded, my heart racing and my mind swirling. I wanted to say no, that stopping by would be impossible, but I couldn't do that. She seemed so excited at the prospect. "I will," I said as I slipped her card into my back pocket.

Hugging her book to her chest, she nodded. "I'll see you later then."

I watched as she hurried down the sidewalk. "See you," I called after her.

She gave me a final wave before rounding the corner and disappearing. I let out the breath I hadn't realized I'd been holding. I made a beeline for the nearest bench and proceeded to collapse on it.

My brain was struggling to process what had happened. I'd just met Spencer's daughter. She was as sweet as she was adorable. She was happy and well-adjusted. I wasn't sure what Spencer was concerned about. In a way, she reminded me of Maggie, and that only made me want to get to know her better.

I opened my bag of fudge, and even though it was only

nine thirty in the morning, I was going to eat it. The stress of this trip was getting to me, and meeting Abigail hadn't helped. If anything, I was now a giant bundle of nerves. I was worried what Spencer would think once he discovered that we'd already met. What if he couldn't bring himself to meet with her? He would effectively stop my relationship with his daughters before it even began.

I sighed. Why did life have to be this complicated?

"Mrs. Brown?"

I startled at the sound of my name. I glanced up to see Colten standing in front of me. He looked confused, but his smile was hard to ignore. Naomi was standing next to him, looking as confused as I was.

"Colten?" I glanced over at Naomi. "Naomi?"

"Yeah, what are you doing here?" Colten asked as he reached out and shook my hand. He laughed. "I had to do a double take to make sure that I wasn't still in Magnolia."

I nodded. "Yeah, what a small world. I'm here with..." Should I say Spencer? What if they wanted to know more? What was I going to say then? I cleared my throat. "Spencer and I are vacationing here." Colten glanced around, and I could see his confusion. Before he could ask me where Spencer was, I hurried to add, "He's still sleeping, that goof."

I winced as my voice sounded desperate even to my own ears. Even though I hated lying, I didn't really have another choice. I kept my smile broad as I glanced between Naomi and Colten. "And you two are?" I raised my eyebrows.

Colten shook his head. "I'm just visiting. Naomi lives here with Walker."

Memories came rushing back. That was right. Walker and Naomi were dating again. Jackson and Fiona had been so broken after she left. I glanced over at her, and she looked uncomfortable. There was something in the way she stood there that reminded me of...me. I'd been in a similar situation before.

I knew the look of a lonely woman like I knew the back of my hand.

"It's good to see you," I said as I stood and pulled her into a hug. Even though we were only acquaintances, I wasn't going to hold back. She looked broken. And broken people craved physical touch, even if they didn't know it.

"You too," she said as she patted my back.

I smiled as I pulled away. "How do you like living here in Harmony?"

She glanced around. "It's good. Walker is out on the rig for the month, so I'm looking for a job." She held up a stack of papers.

"That's too bad," I said.

She looked confused.

I shook my head and offered her an apologetic smile. "Sorry. What I meant to say is that it's too bad that you are here and not in Magnolia. I would have loved to hire you for the paper."

She studied me and then nodded. "Yeah, that's too bad. Walker and I love living here."

I nodded. "I can see why. I've been here a day and I love it." I folded my arms and took in a deep breath. "I love the small-town feel."

"Yeah." She fiddled with the papers.

I could tell that she wanted to get moving. Not wanting to be the reason she felt uncomfortable, I smiled at both of them. "I should get going. I need to get back to Spencer." I took a step in the opposite direction from where they seemed to be heading.

"It was good to see you," Colten said as he raised his hand halfway.

"You too." I turned around and took a few steps. "Maybe we'll get together for dinner sometime?" I asked over my shoulder.

"Sure," Colten said. "I'll get your number from Jackson."

I gave them a smile and then hurried down the sidewalk. Once I rounded the nearby building, I stopped and took a deep breath. Even though I was in a hurry to get away from them, I really had nowhere to go.

Despite what I told Colten and Naomi, Spencer was *not* waiting for me. I wasn't going to meet up with him. In truth, I had no one to meet and nowhere to go.

For the first time since New York, I felt alone. I missed Maggie. I missed Magnolia Daily and Victoria and her pushy personality. I missed the book club and having a group of women that I could call if I needed something.

Here, I knew no one.

I sighed and pushed my hair out of my face. I was going to throw a pity party, and then I was going to put on my big-girl pants and move on. After a few seconds, I squared my shoulders and headed back toward the Apple Blossom B&B.

If I needed a distraction, I knew the perfect person who would keep me so busy that I wouldn't have time to breathe.

I was ready to put myself in Missy's hands.

Heaven help me.

8

NAOMI

It was strange seeing Penny here. We'd only interacted a few times in the past, but seeing her reminded me of Jackson, and for a second, I allowed myself to wonder if he was here as well. But then I felt stupid.

Of course, he wasn't here. He was mad at me and wanted nothing to do with me. So much so that Colten had to come here alone to check on me.

Things had never gotten this bad with Jackson. We'd always managed to make things work. We'd never gone this long without talking. Even though I wanted to pick up the phone and call him, something was holding me back. I didn't need a lecture about Walker, and I didn't need him acting like an overprotective big brother.

Right now, I needed support. I was determined to keep company with people who lifted me up and supported me. And right now, that did not include Jackson.

"You okay?"

I glanced over at Colten, who was walking next to me. I'd lost myself in thought, and I hadn't noticed that he was staring at me with his eyebrows knit together.

I pinched my lips and nodded. I wasn't sure what to say, and the last thing I wanted to do was bring up my strained relationship with my brother. I didn't need Colten calling Jackson and demanding that he come down here. If Jackson wanted to see me, I wanted it to be on his terms, not Colten's.

Plus, if Jackson was going to come down here to demand that I break up with Walker and come back to Magnolia, then he could save it. I wasn't going anywhere. I was determined to be my own boss.

I was tired of Jackson pushing me around.

"I'm fine," I said as I grabbed the application for Godwins out of the pile and headed into the store. It was a strange turn of events that I would rather face Betty than stand on the sidewalk and discuss my complicated relationship with my brother. I wanted to forget that he existed and move on with my life.

Thankfully, Harold was the only one in the store, and he didn't look interested in talking to me. So, I handed him my application, and he took it without saying anything. I headed out of the store and found Colten standing near the entrance. He had his phone out, and his fingers were moving like he was texting someone.

Curiosity got the better of me as I approached him. "Who are you texting?" I asked. For a moment, I feared that it was Jackson, but then I pushed that from my mind. So what if he was? It didn't affect me. There was no way I was going anywhere even if my brother did show up.

I was tired of him being right all the time and me being wrong. I'd let him drag me away once; I wasn't going to do it again.

"My sister," Colten said as he slipped his phone into his pocket.

I paused, glancing at him over my shoulder. "Your sister?"

He nodded as he joined up with me. "She's having some guy trouble, and I'm giving her advice."

"Trinity or Stephanie?"

Colten paused and looked over at me. "You remember my sisters?"

I snorted. "Of course." Was that strange? Colten was a big part of Jackson's life. Even though I'd become distant, my brother and I were normally very close. "I think Trinity had a crush on Jackson for a while. He'd call and ask me what he should do."

Colten stopped walking and turned to stare at me. "Trinity liked Jackson?"

"It was years ago. I'm sure she's over it by now." I

shrugged. "Besides, I'm fairly certain he's going to propose to Fiona, so it doesn't matter now."

Colten turned his focus forward and started walking again. "Still. That's not what I want to hear."

"Why?" I wasn't sure why he was so against it. After all, he knew Jackson. He knew that Jackson was a good guy. What did he have against his sister liking his friend?

"I don't know. I mean, she's my sister, and he's my friend." He sighed. "It would be weird."

"It's weird for your friends to like your family members?" Why was I feeling like he was shutting the door on the possibility of a relationship with me? Even though that was a ridiculous thought, I couldn't help but have it float to the center of my mind.

Colten glanced down at me. "Isn't it weird for you?"

I chewed my bottom lip and shook my head. "I wouldn't say *weird*, per se. If a friend of mine got together with Jackson, I think it would be exciting."

Colten was studying me when my gaze met his. I couldn't read his expression, and I wasn't sure I wanted to. Either way, whatever he was thinking was not what I wanted to hear. I didn't want him to tell me either that family members were off-limits or that there was a chance.

I was with Walker.

"Let's take this one to the bookstore," I said, holding up the application for The Shop Around the Corner, and nodded in the direction we needed to go.

Colten didn't say anything as he followed after me. He remained silent the entire way. Once we got to the store, I took in a deep breath as I peered through the glass door. This was it. If I were honest with myself, this was where I wanted to work. It was like a dream come true. I loved *Beauty and the Beast* growing up, and the thought of working in a bookstore that mirrored the collection that the Beast gave Belle...sign me up.

It was destiny, and no one was going to tell me differently.

"Are you going to open the door?" Colten's voice startled me, and I jumped.

I glanced over to see him lean toward me, his eyebrows raised. Once I regained my composure, I nodded. "Yes. I was just preparing myself."

He frowned. "For what? They told you to apply."

I swatted his arm. "I know that. I just..." I took a deep breath. "I want them to want me."

I could feel Colten's stare as the words left my lips. It was intense and sent shivers down my back. I wanted to look over and meet his gaze, I just feared how it would make me feel. Or what it would mean.

"They'd be stupid not to want you," he whispered.

I knew I shouldn't read into his words—I shouldn't— but I did. My heart began to pound as his words raced through my mind. My body was reacting to his closeness and the tone of his voice. I wanted it to mean something, but I knew I was just being stupid. After all, he'd just finished telling me how he thought it was weird when family members dated friends.

Last I checked, he and Jackson were best friends, and I was Jackson's little sister. It would be smart of me to forget these feelings before I drove myself crazy.

Unable to stand there, analyzing his words and meanings any longer, I grabbed the door handle and pulled. The smell of coffee and baked goods filled the air as I entered. Abigail was sitting behind the counter with her feet pulled up and a book balanced on her lap. She was sipping from a mug that said, *It's Not Hoarding if it's Books,* on the side.

Her gaze rose to study us, and a smile emerged from behind the mug. She finished drinking, slipped in her bookmark, and stood. "Good morning," she said as she set down her mug.

"Morning," I said as I walked in, suddenly feeling incredibly shy. I hated that I felt this way.

Abigail leaned her elbows on the counter and leaned forward. "Did you get the application filled out?" She rose up on her tiptoes to see the paper I was holding.

I nodded, slipping the top sheet off the stack and onto the marble countertop.

She picked it up and ran her gaze over it. "Wonderful." She paused, lingering on something in the middle before glancing up and smiling. "I'll call your references and see what they say." She shrugged. "I'm sure it'll be good."

"It should be fine," I whispered. Despite the fact

that I had to take some time off because of the car accident and moving to Magnolia, I'd worked most of my
life.

She pulled open a drawer behind the counter and set
the paper into it. After she shut it, she looked up. "Do you
two want some coffee?"

I glanced behind me. Colten was standing a few feet
away. I wasn't sure what he wanted, but I knew I could
use some liquid energy. "Sure." Then I raised my hand. "I
mean, if you don't mind."

She shook her head. "I don't mind," she said as she
rounded the corner and leaned in. "It's kind of my job."

I nodded as I followed her over to the small cafe in the
back. There were a few metal tables with heart-shaped
chairs in front of the bright-red counter. She started gathering items from behind it. "I make a mean caramel
macchiato," she said.

I wasn't into flavored coffee, but I didn't want to say
anything. So, I just nodded. "That sounds good."

She smiled and continued moving. "I also just baked a
batch of oatmeal raisin cookies if you'd like one."

My stomach growled. Even though it had only been a
few hours since I ate, I was starving again. I couldn't help
but imagine the baby inside of my stomach, eating all the
food I did. It was the only way I could explain my vora-
cious appetite.

"Perfect. You two can have a seat—I'll bring the food
to you." She waved her hand toward the bookshelves. "Go

ahead and pick out a few books if you want to read while you wait."

I sat in one of the heart-shaped chairs across from Colten and glanced at the shelves. I contemplated getting up, but the truth was, I was tired. Sitting sounded like a dream right now.

"Thanks," Colten said as he moved to stand. He wandered down an aisle and disappeared out of sight.

With him gone, I could relax. I leaned back in the chair and sighed. I was exhausted from the rollercoaster of emotions that I experienced when he was around. I hated that I didn't feel settled when we talked. I hated that he was staying with me. That I questioned my relationship with Walker when Colten was nice to me...when he smiled at me.

I just wanted to feel content, and yet that was the last thing my body wanted to do. I was a nervous wreck constantly, and it was wearing me out.

"So where did you move from?"

Abigail's voice broke into my thoughts, and I turned to face her. She was plating some cookies and glanced up to smile at me.

"Wilmington."

"So close."

I nodded.

"How do you like living in Harmony?"

I glanced toward the large picture windows at the front of the store. The truth was... this place felt perfect.

The town was friendly. The scenery took your breath away. I just didn't feel at home.

Not yet at least.

"It's good. I'm getting used to it still."

She nodded. "And Walker? What does he do?"

I glanced toward Colten, remembering how he felt when I introduced him as Walker. I didn't want him to get mad and storm out again, but I couldn't just ignore Abigail's question. "He likes it here, and he works on an oil rig." I squeezed my eyes shut. Why was I keeping up this lie?

I was fairly certain that Abigail was a smart person. She was going to realize that Colten wasn't Walker when he left to go back to Magnolia and the real Walker appeared next to me. That was especially true if she decided to hire me.

"Are you okay?" Abigail was standing in front of me with the plate of cookies in her hand and a steaming mug of coffee. She set them down and then joined me, pulling in Colten's now vacant chair and resting her elbows on the table.

"Yeah," I said, hating that it seemed as if she could read me. What was my expression saying? That I was a liar?

Ugh. Since when had my life turned into this? I was an emotional wreck, and I was lying to potential friends. Add that to the fact that I was blatantly disregarding my future husband by having my brother's best friend stay with me in our apartment. How had I let it get this bad?

I needed to be better. But I didn't know how to fix any of this.

"It's just a lot. A new town. A new place. A new life." That was true. My whole life felt like a weight on my shoulders. Ever since the accident, I felt as if I was running and running and never catching up.

It was exhausting.

"How do you feel about movies?"

Needing a distraction from my own mind, I picked up my mug and took a sip. Then I glanced over at Abigail as I set it back down. "Like, in general?"

She laughed and shook her head. "Like, as in a thing to do."

Was she asking me to go to the movies with her? "I enjoy them."

Her grin widened. "Tomorrow is discount night at the Harmony Multiplex. Wanna go with me? There's a super cheesy rom-com that everyone is talking about." She leaned in. "I'll buy the popcorn."

I wasn't going to lie. Taking a break from Colten and going out with the girls sounded amazing. "Are you sure?"

She frowned. "Why wouldn't I be sure? You look like you could use a friend, and I know everyone in town. I'm excited to get to know someone new." She leaned in. "You should say yes."

I paused and then smiled. "Okay."

"Okay?" she asked, pulling back.

I nodded. "Okay."

She clapped her hands. "Wonderful. I have your number from your application. I'll text you with times..." Her voice trailed off as her gaze focused on the front windows. She looked confused; her gaze locked on a man who was shuffling to the door. "Why is he here?" she whispered as she moved to stand.

I glanced at the man she was looking at and then back to her. His head was tucked in, and his arms were folded tightly against his chest. "Is everything okay?" I asked, worry brewing in my stomach. Who was this man, and why did he make her look so concerned?

Abigail glanced over at me as if she suddenly realized that I was still here. "Um, yeah. Will you excuse me?" she asked as the man pulled open the front door.

I nodded, my muscles poised to jump up and protect us.

Abigail hurried over to him, and for a moment, I felt as if I were intruding on something. Then the man looked up, and I realized that I recognized him. I wasn't sure from where, but I was fairly certain I knew him.

"Why is Spencer here?"

Colten's voice startled me. I yelped and turned to look at him. "Spencer?" I asked, taking note of the stack of books in Colten's hands.

He nodded as he set them down in front of me. One of

them was titled *What to Expect When You're Expecting*. The other ones were similar.

I swallowed, hating that he was thinking of buying these but secretly melting inside that he'd thought of me. Would Walker have done the same if he knew that I was pregnant? I so desperately wanted to say yes, but deep down, I knew the truth.

He wouldn't.

"He's dating Penny." He frowned. "I thought she was meeting up with him."

I glanced over at Spencer, who was speaking to Abigail in a hushed tone. I didn't want to eavesdrop, but I couldn't curb my curiosity. Was this why they were here? Was he cheating on Penny with Abigail? Or was something else going on?

Why would Penny lie to us?

I felt more confused than ever.

Spencer must have felt us staring at him because suddenly his gaze was on us. As soon as he saw Colten, he backed away from Abigail, who looked extremely distressed. The happy, relaxed woman had her arms folded and her lips pinched.

"I'm so sorry I came," Spencer said before he turned and hurried from the store.

Abigail watched his retreat until he disappeared around the corner. I didn't mean to stare, but it was strange that my new friend knew someone from the town I'd just left.

As if she suddenly realized that we were still sitting there, Abigail turned and forced a smile. "How do the cookies taste?"

Colten and I pulled back, and we each picked up a cookie.

"They're delicious," Colten said through a mouthful.

I chewed and nodded in agreement.

She studied us and then waved toward the door. "Sorry about that. My past just suddenly appeared." Her voice was broken. Such a stark contrast to her previous cheerful demeanor. She glanced toward the windows and then down at her feet. I could tell that she was trying to process something, and I wanted to ask her if she was okay, but I also didn't want to intrude. After all, we'd only just met.

"I have to go make a phone call. Are you guys going to be okay?"

We both nodded in unison.

She paused. "I'll text you later," she said to me as she passed by.

"That's fine," I called over my shoulder. She walked into the back room, and the door swung shut behind her.

The shop fell silent as Colten and I sat there, finishing our cookies. Once we were done, Colten glanced over at me.

"Should we go?" he asked.

I nodded. That was probably the best idea. "I think she might want some privacy."

Colten agreed. We stood, threw away our garbage, stacked the dishes on the counter, and headed out the door. I waited while Colten put a few twenties down next to the register and wrote a list of the books he was buying.

He tucked the books under his arm, and I held the door open for him. I wanted to thank him for buying the books, and I made a mental note to do that later.

As soon as we were outside and the door shut behind us, I glanced over at him. "What do you think that was about?"

He shrugged. "No idea."

9

PENNY

Missy tsked for the tenth time in the last five minutes. I studied her, trying to gauge what I was doing wrong. She had me making wreaths to decorate the lampposts in the center of town, and I seemed to be messing up the wired ribbon that I was wrapping around the metal wreath frames.

What had started out as something to take my mind off of Spencer abandoning me was now stressing me out. I hated to disappoint, but that was all I was currently doing. I'd texted her after my run-in with Abigail, and she'd said she was working with the festival committee at the community center just a few blocks down.

I'd welcomed the distraction earlier, but now, I was regretting my decision. I offered her a weak smile, but she just pinched her lips and narrowed her eyes. I focused back on the wreath as I attempted once more to make large spirals to twist-tie to the frame.

All I ended up doing was smashing the curls.

"Is there something else I can help with?" I asked as I set the ribbon and frame down on the table. "I just don't think I'm a wreath-making person." I gave her a small shrug and an apologetic smile.

Missy placed her hand on her hip as she studied me. "I think you're right, honey." Then she lifted my pathetic attempt. "Bless your heart. At least you tried."

The other women at the table all muttered in agreement. I gave them a guilty smile, feeling ridiculous for thinking I could do this. That I could actually be of help.

Read a mystery and discover plot holes? I had that in the bag. But using my hands to create something that was fluffy and beautiful? Apparently, that was a skill I lacked.

"Why don't you stuff goodie bags with Charlotte?" Missy suggested as she nodded toward the older woman who was sitting in the back of the community center, surrounded by tulle and bowls of candy.

I nodded. That sounded more in my wheelhouse. "Yeah, sure. That sounds great." I headed over to the table and collapsed on the chair opposite the woman.

She jumped and glanced up at me. Then she narrowed her eyes. "Did Lord Missy banish you too?" Charlotte asked as she reached forward and grabbed a handful of candy.

I laughed. "My production wasn't up to her standards," I said as I glanced around, wondering where to even start. Compared to Missy, Charlotte was sloppier. But I kind of liked it. She felt more real.

Charlotte snorted. "No one lives up to her standards."

I leaned forward. "What did you do?"

Charlotte glanced up. Her eyes were dark green and inviting. "The real truth?"

I nodded.

Charlotte sighed as she reached forward and removed a square of tulle from the stack next to her. She laid it in front of me and then waved toward the candy. "Missy and I go back a long ways." Then she pointed toward her white hair pulled back into a bun. "A long, *long* way."

I smiled as I started setting pieces of candy into the center of the square. "So, what did you do?"

"Me, child?" Charlotte asked in a voice that said she was taken back by what I'd insinuated. "I did nothing." She jutted her thumb in Missy's direction. "It was that woman. She's the one who said I stole Branson Cliff from her."

"Branson Cliff?"

"Branson Cliff." She patted her heart with her hand. "If you'd seen the man, you would have fallen in love with him as well."

I could only imagine. "So, you stole him?"

Charlotte snorted. "He asked *me* to the homecoming dance. I stole no one."

I busied myself with tying ribbon around the tulle that

was now full of candy. "So, what happened?" I asked as I set the goodie bag in the growing pile next to her and picked up another square of tulle.

Charlotte smiled as she continued filling her bag. "Well, we went" —she leaned forward and lowered her voice— "we kissed."

I parted my lips into an *o*, raising my eyebrows.

"We dated. Then he went to college, and I stayed home." She sighed. "He found some girl at school, so we broke up." She glanced off to the side like she was trying to remember something. "I think he died a few years back."

That wasn't the ending I'd expected. "Oh. I'm sorry."

Charlotte shrugged. "It's okay. That's what happens when you get old, honey." She set her bag on the stack and started over.

"That seems a little petty to still be angry with you over that." There had to be more to this story than what she was telling me.

Charlotte shrugged. "Don't be fooled by Missy's friendly demeanor. She can turn on you so fast." She raised her arthritic hand and managed a snap. Even though she was most likely thirty years my senior, I was enjoying her immensely. I only wished that I held that same level of spunk when I was her age.

"So, there's more?" I asked.

Charlotte nodded. "I run the Harmony Island Inn on the other side of the island. Ever since I opened, she's waged war on me. Apparently, there can be only one place for people to stay in Harmony."

Missy's anger made more sense. There was nothing that would stir the pot more than competition. I saw it all the time in the publishing world. Wars that were waged because a publisher had to have *the* book.

It was a sad and brutal part of living in a world with other people.

Charlotte sighed, bringing my attention back to her. "And so here I sit. My lot in life is getting all of the crap jobs from Missy." She shrugged. "You know what?"

I shook my head.

"I'm going to do each job to the best of my ability." She shoved her thumb in Missy's direction once more. "I'm not going to let her have the satisfaction of besting me." Then she leaned forward. "Especially when my inn is better than her B&B."

All I could do was smile. I'd never seen the Harmony Island Inn, therefore, I couldn't weigh in. But if it was anything like Charlotte, I was certain I would enjoy it.

She glanced up at me. "You'll have to come visit me sometime, you know, while you're here." She stopped like she was thinking. "Tomorrow would be good. Gareth is making wild rice soup, and it's to die for." Her gaze was back on me, and I could tell she wanted an answer.

I wasn't sure what Spencer had planned for tomorrow, but I was fairly certain it didn't involve me. Still, I needed to keep it open, so I shrugged. "Possibly. I'll have to ask the person I'm here with if he's free."

Charlotte nodded. "Of course." Then she leaned back. "Just stop by any day that works. If you have some free time."

"I will."

We made small chat for the next hour before Missy declared our work done and excused us for lunch. Charlotte stood and moved slowly to the door, where a tall man greeted her. I wondered if that was Gareth and made a mental note to ask her when I saw her next.

I wasn't really interested in eating with Missy, so I pulled my phone from pocket only to feel disappointment wash over me. There was still no contact from Spencer. No text or call.

Besides a few junk emails and a heart emoji from Maggie, my phone was empty.

I sighed, slipping it back into my pocket. Since I wasn't going to stay here, I might as well find a place to get some food. I nodded to Missy and the other women who'd gathered to eat from the large wicker picnic basket she'd laid out on the table.

I didn't stop even though Missy looked as if she were going to say something. Instead, I continued through the door and out into the sun. Even though the fact that Spencer hadn't called still bothered me, I couldn't help but breathe better out here.

I tipped my face toward the sky and closed my eyes.

The warm sun brightened my mood. I was still enjoying myself, even if my heart was breaking over Spencer.

"We meet again." Abigail's voice broke the silence.

I straightened and glanced over at her. Her hands were full of groceries, and she was smiling. She looked a little sadder than she had this morning, and I wondered if Spencer had gone to see her. I wanted to ask, but I knew it was none of my business. And I wanted Spencer to tell me out of his own volition, not because I'd poked around in his business.

"How's it going?" I asked as I eyed her grocery bags.

She lifted them up. "Getting supplies for sandwiches at the store." Then she narrowed her eyes. "You look like a hungry woman. Wanna join me?"

I knew I should have said no. I should have walked away. This was Spencer's battle, not mine. But Abigail looked so earnest as she studied me, and the last thing I wanted was to disappoint her.

So, I nodded. "Sure."

She smiled as she started walking toward the bookstore. I followed alongside her. "Do you want some help?" I asked, nodding toward the bags.

She handed over the bags she held in one hand. "That would be great," she breathed as I took them from her.

Once we were situated with bags evenly distributed, we continued down the street.

"Are you keeping busy?" she asked.

I nodded. "Missy has me making wreaths—scratch

that—she *had* me making wreaths. Now she has me filling goodie bags because I lacked the necessary skills."

Abigail broke out in laughter. "That's Missy for you."

"I'm learning that."

Abigail glanced over at me. "So, besides spending time with Missy, what brought you to Harmony Island?"

We paused at a crosswalk to let a car go by. I tried to think of a plausible reason to be here that didn't involve her father.

"Just visiting. I needed a break from life." That was a total lie. If anything, I loved my job and the life that I'd started in Magnolia. I just knew that having Abigail and Sabrina in our life would make it that much sweeter. And now that I knew she liked books—especially the ones that I'd helped create—I needed her in my life.

Having them visit Spencer and me would be the icing on the cake.

"Where is home?"

"Magnolia, Rhode Island."

She shook her head. "I've never heard of it."

"It's a small island off the mainland."

"Ah." Then she paused. "Have you lived there your whole life?"

I shook my head. "I used to live in New York but moved just a few months ago. My daughter runs the inn there." Abigail glanced over at me. "Long story. It was handed down in my family. Relationship issues caused me to forget it was there. Maggie needed money, so I told her to fix up the inn and sell it. She fell in love with the town and decided to stay."

Now that I was on a roll, I couldn't stop. "She got engaged, and I realized how much of her life I'd missed, so I came to help with the wedding. We reconciled. I lost my job in New York. And now I live there and run Magnolia Daily."

We were at the front doors of the bookstore now. I let out the rest of my breath as Abigail turned to face me.

"That's a lot." She set down her bags and felt around in her purse until she emerged with her keys. "It sounds like it would make a fantastic book."

I laughed. "Yeah, it would."

She pushed open the door and I followed after her. She led me into the small kitchen behind the cafe counter. I set the groceries down and stepped to the back part of the kitchen while she put the cold items in the fridge and the dry items into the cupboard.

"What kind of sandwich would you like?" she asked as she started putting away the deli meat.

"Whatever is easiest. I'm not picky."

She glanced down at the bags and then shrugged. "Ham it is."

"Ham's perfect," I said. "Anything I can do to help?"

She shook her head. "Keeping me company is help enough."

I nodded and found a small stool in the corner. After bringing it closer, I sat down on it. I hated that I was just sitting around. I wanted to help, but Abigail seemed determined to do it on her own. I tried to respect that.

"It's funny that you told me your story," she said, drawing my attention over to her. She was focused on the sandwich she was making like it held the answers to all of life's questions.

"Really?" I'd heard my story referred to as a lot of things, but funny wasn't one of them.

She nodded. "The fact that you were estranged from your daughter but found a way to make amends." Her voice grew quiet, and I could tell that she was deep in thought.

From the way she was talking, it sounded like Spencer had been here. Blast that man for shutting me out. Had he kept me in the loop, I wouldn't be in the dark here.

"Do you have a similar story?" I asked, hoping that I wasn't being rude by asking.

Abigail glanced over at me. She paused before she nodded. "Something like that." She sighed. "And I don't know what to do about it." Her voice was a whisper now.

I could tell she was hurting, and that broke my heart. I knew what that was like. My relationship with Dorthy had always been strained, and it had definitely continued through to Maggie.

I'd spent my whole life running from relationships and, in turn, hurting those I cared about. If I could impart any of my wisdom, I was going to. I wanted her to live her life without regret.

"I'm happy to listen if you want," I offered, shrugging my shoulders and offering her a small smile.

She studied me and then returned to slathering the bread with mayonnaise. She was quiet, and I worried that I'd overstepped. That I'd ruined this relationship before it even started.

"My mom died a little over twenty-five years ago."

"I'm so sorry."

She glanced up at me. "Yeah. It was hard. I was a little girl, and it was hard being raised by my dad."

I nodded. Spencer now hadn't been shy about the fact that he'd struggled to be a dad to his girls after Rosalie died. It was one of his biggest regrets. If only she would listen to him, I knew he would apologize. I knew he would take responsibility for everything that he did.

But from the lack of his presence, he either hadn't come by, or she hadn't let him in. Both scenarios made me sad for them.

However, I understood the reasons why either Spencer or Abigail was holding back. They were scared, and time was the only thing to heal those wounds.

"Do you still have a relationship with him?" I asked.

She shook her head. Which meant that Spencer hadn't come to see her. Then her shake slowly turned to a nod. "We hadn't talked in ten years," she whispered, "until he showed up this afternoon."

He had been here. "He showed up today? What happened?" Was I being too pushy? Would she realize that I knew her dad? I hoped I wasn't making a mistake by playing dumb.

She nodded. "Yeah. Like, out of the blue. I didn't think he even knew where we were." She turned and leaned against the countertop with one arm folded across her chest. "I don't even know where he's been hiding out." She glanced over at me. "Isn't that strange? Why today of all days?"

I shrugged. "Sometimes, things eat at a person, and suddenly they act."

She stared off in front of her, and I could see that she was trying to process Spencer's actions. I wanted to tell her that if she figured out her dad, to let me know, but I decided to keep that to myself. That could be a conversation we had after she knew who I was.

She blinked a few times and then returned to the sandwiches. "I guess. But it was strange. So much so that I didn't know what to say to him. I just told him to leave." She sighed. "I don't even know what to say to Sabrina, my sister. She's pregnant and it's high risk. I'm worried she'll go into premature labor if she finds out."

"Really?" I hadn't even thought of that. I knew that Spencer would never want to hurt his daughters.

"Sabrina took it harder when Mom died. Even though I'm the younger sister, I've always protected her."

"I get that." One of my biggest regrets was that Maggie never had a sibling to talk to. To lean on. I wished I had given her that, but time wasn't on my side. "You know what, take your time." I gave Abigail a soft smile. "If he comes back, try to listen to what he has to say. Then take your time to think about what he proposes. Sometimes, we just need to say something. To get if off our chest. I'm sure he's not expecting everything to be fixed in an afternoon."

Abigail opened a drawer and pulled out a kitchen knife. After cutting the sandwiches in half and plating them, she handed one over to me. "Chips are in the cupboard behind you."

I thanked her.

Even though I wanted to talk more about Spencer, Abigail seemed ready to move the conversation in a different direction. I followed her as she led the way into the bookstore and settled down on a chair.

Spencer never came up again. Instead, we chatted about books and shared our favorite passages. By the end, we were laughing and had a stack of books on the table next to us.

I didn't linger too long after helping Abigail clean up. I knew Missy was expecting me back, and I didn't want to face her wrath. Just before I slipped out of the bookstore, I wrote a small note telling Abigail that I enjoyed lunch and left a twenty to pay for it.

As I walked back to the community center, I couldn't help but smile. I was grateful for the time I spent with her. I was getting to know her on a deeper level and possibly helping Spencer get his foot in the door.

Even though there was a part of me that worried what

would happen when she found out who I was, I decided to push that out of my mind.

Whatever happened, I would face it.

For today, I'd enjoy what I had. I would live in the present. I'd live for the happiness I felt.

I would worry about everything else tomorrow.

10

NAOMI

W e made it back to my apartment an hour later, which was a good thing. My feet were starting to swell, and my hip was giving me more aches than it had in a while. I was ready for a long soak in the tub and curling up on the couch with a blanket and a show.

Colten seemed to feel the same. He had his shoes off and was headed into the kitchen like he was going to start dinner. I honestly didn't care. If he cooked, that would save me from having to make any food or order out.

If he wanted to take on the cooking in our relationship, I wasn't going to stop him.

"I think I'm going to take a bath," I said as I moved to lean against the nearest counter. I slid my hands across the cool stone until I was far enough forward to take the pressure off my hips. My stomach felt weighed to the ground, but I didn't care. My hip was hurting me.

From the corner of my eye, I saw Colten turn to face me but stop in his tracks. I could feel his gaze on me, and his expression looked startled. My skin warmed from his gaze, but it didn't last long. A few seconds later, he turned back to the cupboard he'd been exploring.

Not sure what his look meant, and certain that I didn't want to see it again, I pushed off the counter and stretched my arms over my head as I moved toward the master bedroom. "I'll be out in thirty minutes at the minimum," I called over my shoulder before shutting the door behind me.

I padded over to the bathtub and started the water. After plugging the tub, I added some bath salts. Then I went to my room to slip out of my clothes and gather a towel for when I was finished.

The water was perfect by the time I got back into the bathroom, so I slipped in gingerly. I was achy, but the temperature took a moment to get used to. I was submerged up to my tummy, but my baby bump was a few inches above the water line. I tipped my head back and closed my eyes. Soft instrumental music played from my phone.

I allowed my mind to clear as I focused on relaxing my body and listening to the music. Even though my mind started to wander into uncharted territory involving Colten and me, I instantly pushed those thoughts out. This wasn't the time or place to psychoanalyze the looks he gave me or the way he stared at me like he appreciated the view.

The truth was, he was never going to see me like I wanted him to see me. He'd admitted that himself in no uncertain terms.

I shook my head in an effort to dispel the thoughts that were trying to weasel themselves into my head. I pinched my eyes shut, hoping that would help.

It didn't.

Colten was in my head whether I wanted him there or not. I might as well charge him rent if he was never going to leave.

Groaning, I moved to sit up. I dried off my hand and grabbed my phone. It had only been ten minutes since I'd climbed into the tub, and I was no more relaxed than when I'd started.

Frustrated, I forced myself to sit there for a few more minutes before I declared this bath a mistake and pulled the plug. I placed my hands on either side of the tub and started to push myself up. But as I did, my foot slipped out from under me, and suddenly I came crashing down onto my bad hip.

I yelled out in pain. Black and white flashes of pain shot through my body and into my eyes. I pinched my eyes shut as I tried to stabilize my body. Thankfully, I didn't land on my stomach, but I was worried.

"Naomi?" Colten's panicked voice sounded from the other side of the bathroom.

I winced when I heard it. I hated that this had happened. I didn't need him worrying about me. And I certainly didn't need him coming into the bathroom when I was naked.

"I'm okay," I wheezed out as I attempted to stand once more. Pain shot down my leg when I tried to apply pressure on my hip. This time, I lowered myself down safely and opened my eyes.

What was I going to do? I wanted to tell Colten that I was fine, and he could go about his business, but I doubted that I would be able to get out anytime soon. He was going to notice if an hour passed and I was still in the tub.

I could either ask him for help or die in a bathtub. I glanced around. Maybe dying wouldn't be so bad.

My hand instinctively found its way to my stomach. My fingers rested on the bump. Maybe I could die in the tub, but I didn't want that for my baby. I was sure the baby was fine, but it was probably best for me to get out.

"I need help," I called out before I could stop myself.

I heard the doorknob turn and the sound of the latch disengaging. The door opened a few centimeters.

"Did you say you need help?" Colten's voice was low, like he was worried he'd overstepped.

My hands went to my visible goods, and I glanced back at the door. "You can come in."

The door swung open all the way, and Colten appeared with his hand clamped over his eyes. "I can come in?" he repeated.

"I tried to get out of the tub and slipped, hitting my hip on the tub. It hurts too much, and I can't get out." I felt like an idiot, sitting there in an empty tub, freezing my butt off while Colten felt his way along the wall as he walked closer.

"There's a towel a few inches to your left. Grab it and throw it directly in front of you."

Colten was quick to obey. When he found the towel, he chucked it in my direction. It hit the wall and landed on my body. I quickly shook it out and tucked it around myself as best I could.

"You can look now," I said, turning my attention back to Colten.

He hesitated but then slowly lowered his hand. His eyes remained clamped shut as he tipped his face toward me. "Are you sure?"

"Yes. I'm covered."

He peeked through one eye, and then both were open. He glanced down at me and then up to the ceiling. He blushed. I couldn't help but smile until his gaze drifted back down to mine.

"What do you need me to do?" he asked as he moved closer to the tub.

I hated how warm my body felt when Colten's gaze ran over me. I wondered if he was experiencing the same thing—then shook that thought from my head. That was wrong on so many levels.

"Just help me out of the tub," I said softly. I didn't have

the strength to get out of the tub, and I certainly didn't have the strength to fight the attraction I felt for Colten. It was too exhausting to ignore, and when I was this tired, my inhibitions were zero.

There was a chemistry between us that I couldn't ignore anymore. I would endure it until he left, and then I wouldn't worry about it. It would be a distant memory as Walker and I moved forward with our life and our baby.

"Is the baby okay?" Colten asked, his gaze resting on my stomach.

I nodded, hating the way his voice softened when he talked about the baby. Or the way he looked at me like I was fragile. I wanted Walker to care about me that much. The fear that he wouldn't was real and tangible. I was afraid I would compare Walker to Colten now that I knew what it was like to have someone who openly cared about me.

Needing to redirect my thoughts, I focused on Colten and what he'd asked me. "I think it's fine. I landed on my hip, and I'm not getting any cramping." I shivered. "I'm just cold."

That spurred Colten into action. Suddenly, he was in front of me, bending down into the tub. He tucked an arm under my knees, and the other one he wrapped around my back. I wanted to tell him that he could just help me balance so I could step out of the tub, but I was airborne before I could gather my thoughts enough to protest.

He tucked me in next to his chest. I could feel the warmth of his body as it pressed against mine. His heart was pounding against my arm, and I was going to choose to believe that it was because of physical exertion instead of anything else.

After all, he saw me as his best friend's little sister, and thinking of me as anything else was, and I quote, "weird." So, these feelings of attraction had to be one-sided.

I was an idiot for allowing these thoughts to bloom into full-blown ridiculousness.

Needing to keep my thoughts clear, I clung tightly to my towel as he carried me from the bathroom to the bedroom. I was fairly certain my derriere was hanging out, and I prayed that he hadn't looked in the mirror as we walked by. Thankfully, he zeroed in on my bed. When he got to the edge, he leaned forward, and I braced myself for him to let me down. Just as he stepped forward, suddenly, I was falling to the bed—along with Colten.

We landed on the bed together, Colten bracing himself above me. His chest was centimeters from mine and rested on my fisted hands as I clung to my towel. His gaze met mine as he stared down at me.

Time slowed to a halt. All I could see was Colten. All I could hear was our breath and the pounding of my heart. All I could feel was his body pressed against mine, warming me at every point of contact.

"Are you okay?" he asked as his gaze roamed my face.

It stopped for a moment on my lips, and I wondered if that had been intentional or if I had an injury there. Out of instinct, I bit my lower lip in an effort to conceal it.

"I think so," I whispered, fairly certain that I wasn't going to be able to talk louder than this. It wasn't only because he was on top of me, but also because my heart was thrumming now. My desire for Colten was growing stronger than I wanted to admit.

Yet with him this close, that desire was hard to ignore.

His gaze returned to mine, and I felt his fingers reach up to brush aside my hair. I pulled my gaze from him, hoping to gather my strength enough to pull away, but when I looked at him again, that will disappeared.

His gaze had turned serious, and I could feel a want in the background. A want that was as palpable as the room around me. A want that had me curious to know more. Even though I knew I shouldn't want more.

And then he was moving. He lowered his head down until our lips were almost touching. My breath caught in my throat as I waited for him to close the distance.

I wanted to kiss Colten.

But it never came. Instead, he stopped and pulled back. There was turmoil in his gaze.

His jaw clenched as he held my gaze, and then a moment later, he was gone. He pushed himself off of me and disappeared from view.

"I'll be in the living room," he said as he pulled the

door shut. The sound of the latch engaging echoed in the room.

I was frozen for the better part of five minutes. All I could do was breathe in and out as the memory of Colten so close to me—so close to kissing me—replayed in my mind. Had he meant to do that? What did it mean?

I groaned as I let go of my towel and draped my arm over my eyes. I'd officially gone crazy.

What was worse was that I wanted him to kiss me. I wanted him to kiss me so bad. The feelings inside of me were impossible to ignore. Yet I feared that I was the one who had roped him into almost kissing me. What if he could feel my attraction to him and that had caused him to act?

What if he really had no intention of seeing me as anyone other than Jackson's little sister, and yet, here I was, drawing him in and making him act in ways he never would have.

I was such a fool.

My leg ached, but I was gaining my strength back as I hobbled around my room to dress. The last thing I needed was to have Colten come back in to check on me and find me lying there, not moving. He'd think I was crazy. I'd had enough of these encounters with him to know that if I continued down this path, I was going to *be* crazy.

I slipped on a pair of pajamas and then hobbled back into the bathroom. I ran a brush through my hair and pulled it up into a ponytail. I needed to look as ho-hum as possible if I was going to keep Colten at a distance.

Once I was dressed, I made my way out to the living room. Colten was finishing up dinner, so I headed to the recliner in the corner to put up my feet.

My body was achy and tired as I lowered myself down into the chair. If Colten knew that I was out of my room, he didn't acknowledge me. His focus was on the food in front of him, which I was grateful for. I needed space from his intense gaze and the feelings that emerged every time he looked at me.

The smell of garlic toast and marinara sauce filled the air, and my mouth began to water. I was ready to eat when he set a plate on the side table next to me and then went back to get his own. I dug in, savoring the taste of tomatoes and herbs on my tongue.

I must have either been extremely hungry or Colten was a master chef, because this was the best meal I'd had in a long time.

It was probably a bit of both.

We finished eating and I set my plate down next to me. Colten stood and grabbed my plate and headed into the kitchen. I watched him unload the dishwasher and move around the kitchen as he cleaned up.

It was strange. Walker never took the initiative to clean up the house. He would always do it once I nagged him enough, though.

Was this normal, or was Colten an anomaly? Did most men help out around the house? Was Walker the strange one?

I felt so confused, and I hated it. Comparing Colten to Walker made my stomach twist. Why didn't things make sense anymore? Why was it so hard for me to read Colten and make a decision?

I closed my eyes and tipped my head back. I needed to sleep. Sleep would help me think better. It would push these spiraling thoughts out of my head, and I could focus.

The sound of Colten moving around in the kitchen stopped, and I peeked through the slit of one eye to see what he was doing. He looked lost in thought as he stared out the kitchen window. Then he shook his head and glanced in my direction.

I quickly closed my eye, hoping he hadn't caught me staring.

"I'm going to bed," he said as he headed over to the couch.

I nodded. He had the right idea. Sleep and space would give us both a break from whatever had happened. "Okay," I said as I pushed myself out of the chair. Just as I hobbled past him, he reached out and grabbed my hand gently.

"Are you okay?" His voice was deep as he slowly brought his gaze up to mine.

In reality, no, I wasn't. Not only because my hip hurt,

but because I was completely confused as to what I wanted from Walker. From Colten.

I wished my life was simpler. That I was happier.

But I was far away from that becoming a reality.

"I'll be okay," I whispered, hating that my skin was reacting from Colten's touch. My hand was warm, and little zaps of electricity were pulsing up my arm. I wanted to lean in. I wanted more than what he was giving me.

He studied me for a moment and then dropped his hand. He lay back on the couch and rested his hands behind his head, closing his eyes.

I studied him for a moment, wondering if he was going to continue. I sighed and made my way to the hallway.

"Good night, Naomi."

I glanced over my shoulder. "Good night, Colten."

He didn't move. Instead, his lips tipped up into a smile. "Sleep tight, don't let the bed bugs bite."

As much as I wanted to fight it, I smiled back. "You, too."

Once I was in my room, I shut the door and let my breath out. Then I made my way over to the bed and braced myself as I pushed my feet against the bed frame so I could lift my body onto the mattress.

I snuggled under the covers and closed my eyes, allowing my body to slip into the warmth and softness of the mattress. My mind swirled, but I pushed those thoughts and fears down.

I'd worry about them tomorrow. For now, I was going

to sleep. And hopefully, if I was lucky, I would not dream about Colten.

But I'd never been a particularly lucky person. I braced myself for Colten's inevitable invasion of my thoughts until tomorrow morning.

Wonderful.

11

PENNY

I was exhausted when I got back to the Apple Blossom B&B at seven that night. My feet hurt, and my back hurt. Charlotte and I had filled the goodie bags, and I spent the rest of the evening cutting paper confetti. There was a moment when I wondered if Missy had just given us some busy work because she didn't want Charlotte and me to mess up the other decorations. But Charlotte assured me that Missy scattered every table with confetti to a nauseous level.

So, I gave it my all.

Thankfully, I wasn't hungry. Missy had the local diner bring in food, and they packed the table with roasted turkey, gravy, and mashed potatoes. It tasted like Thanksgiving, and I may have gorged myself more than I cared to admit.

Without the need for dinner, I could bypass the dining

room and any small talk and head straight up to our room. I didn't see Spencer as I passed by the open rooms, which made me wonder if he was upstairs already.

Panic set in.

Would he know that I spent lunch with Abigail? How would he feel about that?

I doubted he would be happy. After all, he'd made it pretty clear that he didn't want me involved with their relationship. Even though Abigail initiated the connection, I didn't say no.

In some way, I felt I was betraying Spencer even if that wasn't my intention.

When I got to our door, I stood outside of it for a moment, taking in deep breaths to prepare myself for whatever would happen on the other side. Then, feeling like an idiot, I grabbed my key out of my purse and slipped it into the lock.

The lights were low when I walked in. I shut the door quietly and slipped off my shoes and hung my purse on the hook meant for coats. I tiptoed into the room and glanced around the corner.

Spencer was sitting on the bed. He had his glasses on, and he was reading.

"Hey," I said as I made my way to my charger and plugged my phone in.

He looked up at me and then back to his book. "Hey."

This was not going great. How long was he going to be like this? I wanted to ask him, but I feared what he would say. Things were becoming strained in our relationship, and there was nothing I could do to fix it.

Was this the end of us?

The desire to fight filled my gut, so I pushed those thoughts out. No matter what, I wasn't going to leave. I would stay here with him even if he wanted me to leave.

He had no choice. He wasn't going to get rid of me that fast. I just needed to remember that I could be as stubborn as he was.

"How did things go today?" I asked with my back turned to him as I fished out a water bottle from the mini fridge. I didn't look at him when I stood up and cracked the top of the bottle.

"Fine."

I sighed softly. This was going to be so fun. Talking to him was like pulling teeth. Painful and methodical.

"I spent my day with Missy. She had me filling goodie bags and punching out confetti all day." I rolled my shoulders, feeling the stress that had settled there from being hunched over the table. "That woman is a beast."

From the corner of my eye, I saw Spencer nod even though he'd returned his attention to his book. "I can see that."

"She paired me with Charlotte, who apparently owns the Harmony Island Inn. She invited us over for a meal sometime." I shrugged. "It might be fun to go."

Spencer didn't respond, so I continued. "Apparently, Charlotte and Missy have a history, and it's a sordid one." I paused. "Although I'm fairly sure that Missy would have a sordid history with just about anyone. I can see her as someone who rubs just about everyone she meets the wrong way." I shrugged. "She did with me."

Spencer grunted to let me know that he heard me, but he didn't respond or add anything.

I moved to the mirror to make it look like I was studying my own reflection when, in reality, I was watching Spencer.

"What about you? Did you..." My voice trailed off, and I wondered if I should ask what I so desperately wanted to know. Did he talk to Abigail? How had it gone? I'd heard part of her side of the situation, and I wanted to know his.

He flicked his gaze up to me and held it for a moment. I offered him a soft smile with the hope that he would realize I didn't mean to pry or hurt him. I just wanted him to know that I was here to help him through this.

"Did I meet with the girls?" He finished for me as he moved his attention back to his book.

"Yeah." I settled down on the chair so that I could face him.

I could tell that he'd stopped reading even though his gaze was fixed on the pages in front of him. I'd been around Spencer long enough to know when he was thinking things through, and that was what he was doing right now.

"I stopped by Abigail's store," he finally said as he moved to turn the page of his book.

When he didn't add more information, I leaned forward. "And?"

He glanced up at me. "And?"

"How did it go?" Was he really going to make me pull the answer out of him?

He returned his attention back to his book. "It was the first step."

So, it hadn't gone well. With his cryptic words and what I gathered from Abigail, it had been a struggle. Which I had anticipated. After all, he didn't give his daughters any heads-up that he was coming. He just showed up at their work after years of no contact.

It couldn't have been easy for either party.

"So, what's the plan?" I asked as I fiddled with the complementary notepad on the desk next to me.

"Plan?"

I nodded and glanced back at him. "Tomorrow? What are you going to do tomorrow?"

He paused, staring off into the distance as if this wasn't something he'd thought of. Then he turned another page. "I don't know if there will be a tomorrow."

I stood, his words confusing me. I needed to pace. That's when I got my best thinking done. "You haven't thought of where you will go from here?" I stopped to stare at him. "You can't just leave their lives now that you came back. That will crush them." I started pacing again.

"She's testing you. You left before, and she's seeing how far she can push you until you leave again."

My emotions caught in my throat when I thought about everything I'd done to Maggie. She deserved so much better than I'd given her. If I could go back, I would, but I couldn't. At least now, I could stop Spencer from doing the same to his daughters. In a way, if I could mend Spencer's family, it would make up for the lack that had existed in mine.

Spencer's gaze had returned to his book, but I could tell that he wasn't reading. He was thinking. There was something both terrifying and calming about his reaction. It was nice that he was taking into consideration what I'd said, but on the other hand, I had no idea what he was going to say.

I couldn't help but feel as if I were on the razor's edge. Any minute now, he was going to stand up and declare our relationship over. He was going to demand I leave, and I would go back to Magnolia brokenhearted and empty-handed.

The anticipation was killing me.

Spencer never responded. Instead, he shrugged and returned to reading, completely blocking me out. I swallowed as tears formed in my eyes. I wanted him to fight me. I wanted him to get angry. There was nothing more heartbreaking than getting shut out.

I wasn't sure how to fix it or how to make things better.

Instead, I was in the dark. I had no idea what the future would hold, and it was a crappy place to be.

I didn't want to let him know how he was making me feel—after all, I'd been opening up to him to no avail. So, I grabbed my pajamas and clean underwear and headed into the bathroom.

Steam filled the room as I stepped into the hot shower. Once I was drenched, I let the tears flow. My heart was breaking for numerous reasons, and I cried for all of them.

I cried for the hurt I put my own daughter through. I cried for Spencer and his daughters. I cried for the fact that they lost their mom. I cried for the uncertainty of their future.

But most of all, I cried for myself. I cried for my broken heart and my fear that things might not get better with Spencer.

What had started out feeling like a beginning was rapidly becoming an ending.

Were we finished? Had Spencer and I run our course? I wanted to say no, I really did. I wanted to think that we could weather this storm. I would wake up tomorrow, and everything would be back to normal. But I knew that wasn't reality.

Reality was Spencer fixing his relationship with his daughters without me. Reality was the inevitable collapse of our relationship.

As much as I wanted to be angry, I couldn't be. I loved

Spencer, and as a result, I loved his daughters. That was what mattered here.

And I'd step away if I had to.

I didn't want to, but that didn't matter. I'd do it.

No matter what.

12

NAOMI

I'd been right.

Colten invaded my dreams, and no matter how many times I awoke and tried to shake him from my mind, as soon as I slipped into darkness, his face floated to the forefront of my mind. It was both glorious and painful at the same time.

When I finally peeled myself off my mattress at 7:02 the next morning, I was exhausted. I needed a hot shower and a tall glass of water before I would feel alive.

Steam had filled the bathroom when I pulled open the shower curtain and stepped out onto the plush rug. I wrapped a towel around my body and reached forward to wipe the condensation off the mirror.

My hair was slick against my head, and some leftover mascara was smeared under my eyes.

Wonderful.

I looked like a pregnant, crazed person.

I hurried to fix my hair and makeup. After I looked a little more sane, I hobbled into my bedroom to get dressed.

I'd given up pretending that I didn't care what I looked like in front of Colten. It was obvious that I did, and it was too tiring to act otherwise. I was trying not to feel bad about it. After all, he was leaving in a few days. Once he was gone, he would live in the dark corners of my mind for the rest of my life.

Once he was gone, I could go back to pretending I was happy with Walker.

"I'm tired of pretending," I whispered as I sat down on the bed and shoved my legs into my pants. As I pulled them up, I stopped.

They no longer fit.

I stood and shuffled over to the floor-length mirror in my closet. My belly felt as if it had grown overnight. It was protruding so far out, that the opening of the pants wouldn't wrap around it much less allow me to button them closed.

I tried to make the ends meet. I was determined to fix this, but no amount of finagling fixed what had happened. I needed maternity clothes.

I let out a growl and moved into my closet.

I was excited about the baby—I was—but I was going to have to fess up to Walker in the near future. And I wondered what he would say to me about it.

Would he be happy?

Sad?

Would he react like Colten?

I groaned as I closed my eyes and tipped my head back. Why was I doing this? Why was I thinking about Colten?

I was beginning to fear that I couldn't go an hour without thinking about him. If that was the case, what was I going to do once he left? Was I actually going to be able to forget him?

Not wanting to slide down that slippery slope, I grabbed a stretchy maxi dress and pulled it on. After a quick look in the mirror to make sure I looked put together, I headed out to the kitchen.

Colten wasn't there. It was strange that I'd gotten so used to him cooking meals for me. It felt like a hole in my life had opened up when I saw that the lights were off and I wasn't greeted by the smell of fresh bacon and eggs.

I glanced over to the couch to see that it too was empty. My gaze wandered over to the guest bathroom, but the door was open, and no lights were on.

Had he left?

"Colten?" I called out. Our apartment was small. It wasn't like he had a lot of places to go.

There was no answer.

I headed over to the bathroom. After checking behind the shower curtain, I came up empty-handed.

My throat began to tingle with emotions. I hadn't realized until now how I would feel when he left.

I didn't like it.

I wanted to be able to prepare myself for him leaving. I wanted to be able to say goodbye.

This was becoming reminiscent of what I went through when Walker had disappeared on me.

Was this my fate? Were men always going to leave me?

What was so unlovable about me that men could leave without caring about what I would think or how I would feel?

A tear slipped down my cheek, and I winced. I collapsed on the couch and buried my face in my hands. It was true. Everything I feared about myself was true. After all, Walker was supposed to be my fiancé, and Colten... well, he was supposed to be my friend and confidant.

Both men were supposed to stay by me, yet it seemed so easy for them to leave me.

Tears were flowing now. I wanted them to stop. I wanted to be stronger than this, but I couldn't gather myself together enough to control my emotions.

I was breaking.

"Naomi?"

Colten's soft voice caused me to look over.

He was standing next to me with bags of groceries in each hand.

As soon as I saw him, I couldn't stop myself. I stood and wrapped my arms around him, pulling myself close to his chest. He paused for a moment before I heard the bags slip to the ground and his hands were on my waist. He pressed me against him as his arms wrapped around me.

I rose up on my tiptoes, so I could rest my cheek on his shoulder. He rested his cheek next to mine, and I could feel his warm breath on my skin.

I never wanted to be alone again. I was scared of my future, and I was tired of worrying that I would have to face it all alone. Walker was gone, and I wasn't sure if he was coming back. Sure, he told me he had to work, but he'd said that before.

As much as I wanted to tell myself that I hadn't heard that woman on the other end of the phone call the night of my accident, I knew that was a lie. I'd heard her. She was real.

And I still didn't know who she was.

But Colten? I trusted him.

He was always there for me. Protecting me. Making me feel important.

On his vacation, he came to spend time with me. I never felt like I was a burden to him. Like I was just an off-ramp to what he really wanted in life.

"I thought you left," I whispered, closing my eyes and tightening my grip.

"I just went to get some groceries since you were out."

I nodded. After seeing the bags of food, I knew my fear had been unfounded. But it didn't change the fact that I'd allowed myself to believe he would leave.

He was quiet for a moment before he pulled back. I didn't look at him right away. Instead, I focused on the ground. I wanted to come across as strong, but I was certain I looked like a mess.

There was no way that my makeup wasn't smeared and running. I wanted to pretend that I looked amazing, but I knew the truth.

When I finally felt brave enough to meet his gaze, my breath caught in my throat. He was staring at me in a way that was hard to ignore. He wanted me to know that he meant what he was about to say.

"I would never leave without telling you." His voice was deep and growly. I loved it.

I chewed on my bottom lip to keep my focus on his words and not his lips. Memories of how close we got to kissing last night washed over me. I wanted to kiss him. That desire grew to a raging fire inside of my stomach. It surprised and overtook me. I blinked, forcing those thoughts from my mind. That wasn't what I was supposed to be thinking about right now.

"I'm sorry," I whispered as I took a step back. "I think my pregnancy hormones got the better of me. Plus, I was having some flashbacks..." My voice trailed off when Colten frowned.

"Flashbacks?" he asked.

I hadn't wanted to tell him the details when it came to Walker and me. I wanted to put those fears behind me and focus on the future. Apparently, I was a glutton for punishment. Plus, I didn't want Colten to think badly of Walker if I could help it.

"Yeah, Walker left for the rig the night that I got into the accident. He hadn't said anything, though, so I thought he'd left me. And I went out to find him." Even though I wanted to lie and tell him that it didn't matter, I knew that I couldn't do that. I wanted Colten to trust me.

"You drove to go find him even though there was a chance that he could have been on the rig?"

I knew that Colten would see right through my story. He knew I wasn't telling him the whole truth.

"I got a phone call."

He frowned. "A phone call?"

I might as well keep talking. "It was a woman. The conversation was short, and it ended with her hanging up. But it..." I took a deep breath. "It rattled me."

Colten's frown morphed into a glare. "A woman?" he asked, his voice deepening. I could hear the threat in his tone.

I nodded.

"His woman?" Colten scrubbed his face. "Was he cheating on you?"

I wasn't sure what I was supposed to say to that. The truth was I didn't know. I'd come to the same conclusion when I heard her voice on the other end of the line that night, but I'd never spoken to Walker about it. I knew I should have confronted him at some point, but I was scared.

What if it was true? What did that mean for us? For our family?

"You don't know, do you?" The anger had left Colten's voice. All that remained was pity.

Pity for me. Pity for my situation. I hated that. I turned my back to him. I didn't want him to see that I'd failed. So much of my life was in shambles, and I was just trying to hold onto what I could.

I didn't respond, and Colten didn't speak either. A deafening silence fell around us. My ears were ringing from the words that weren't being said. I wanted him to say something. *I* wanted to say something. The trouble was, I didn't know what to say.

"Are you happy?"

I jumped and turned to look at him. He was staring down at me, his gaze asking more than that simple question. His voice sent shivers down my spine.

What was I supposed to say to that? It was a question I'd been refusing to ask myself; how was I going to answer him?

"What?" I asked as I folded my arms across my chest. It was an act of self-preservation. I wanted to hold in the pain that seemed to be seeping from my body. The uncertainty of my life was coming to a head, and I was rapidly losing control of what little I actually had control over.

"Are you happy?" he asked again.

I frowned.

"It's a simple yes or no question, Naomi. Are you happy?"

Why did he keep saying it like that? It wasn't simple. Nothing about my life was simple anymore. Sure, I could pretend. With Walker away, I could pretend that we were just a big, happy family. That everything around me was fine and I was living the life I wanted to live.

It was a lie, but that didn't matter. What else did I have?

"Sure," I finally responded. It was weak and pathetic, but that was all I could give him.

He stepped closer to me. "Really?"

I stepped back, hating that he could read my thoughts. "Really."

He folded his arms across his chest. "I don't believe you."

I scoffed. "Well, it's the truth."

He shook his head. "No, it's not."

I threw up my hands, exhausted from this back and forth. "It's not? Okay, then what is the truth?"

He frowned. "You are not happy."

I met his gaze, tears forming once more on my lids. I wanted to be strong, but I was so tired. Mentally, physically, emotionally. These last few months had taken a toll on me. One that I hadn't predicted, and one that I failed to conquer at every turn.

"What am I then?" I finally asked.

Colten paused, his gaze slipping to the floor as if he were gathering his thoughts. Then he glanced back up. "You're lonely. You're scared." He reached out, his fingertips centimeters from my arm.

But they never made contact. He remained in the same spot, his entire body frozen. I wanted him to touch me. There was a part of me that hoped a touch was all it would take to wake me up. To pull me from this haze I'd been in. To finally get me to act.

I needed that show of strength from someone besides me. If I could rely on Colten, then I might be able to find my way out of this darkness.

The touch never came. Instead, he stared down at his fingers and slowly rolled them into his palm before dropping his hand. Our unspoken words lingered in the air as if we'd said them out loud. I could feel the tension in the room as palpably as if Colten had touched me.

We weren't saying the things we needed to say, and I wondered how long we would last being this close together without speaking. I feared that ruining our relationship would be an unintended consequence. I wasn't ready to deal with that.

Just then, a loud, shrill noise cut through the silence. I startled, and my gaze snapped to my phone on the counter. Realizing that I was being given a chance to escape from whatever was happening between Colten and me, I stepped forward and slipped the phone from the counter.

It was a local number that I didn't recognize. I gave Colten a sheepish smile as I nodded toward the phone and then swiped to answer the call.

"Hello?"

"Naomi? This is Abigail."

I paused. I recognized the name but wasn't sure where from.

"From the bookstore."

"Right! Hi!" I said as I turned my back to Colten.

"I wanted to give you a call and let you know that I talked to my sister, and we want to hire you. We'd need you to work on the weekends and then a few days during the week if that's okay."

I nodded along with each word. I would make it work. "That sounds perfect."

"Great. If you can stop by sometime today, I have some papers for you to sign—you know, tax stuff. I'll give you a tour, and we'll talk hours."

"Perfect. I'll get ready and head down there."

"Wonderful. I'll have a pot of coffee on for you as well."

I was already feeling jittery from my encounter with Colten, and I doubted adding caffeine to that would help. But I wasn't going to turn down free coffee. Especially since she was giving me a job.

We said our goodbyes, and I hung up. I slipped my

phone into my purse as I avoided Colten's gaze. The last thing I needed was to get confused once more.

"I've gotta go," I said, giving him a quick smile.

"Oh, okay."

I could feel his gaze follow me as I collected my shoes and purse. "I don't know when I'll be back, but you'll be okay being alone here, right?"

"Yeah," he said.

From the corner of my eye, I saw him nod and look around.

For a moment, I thought about asking if he wanted to come with me. I wasn't sure if I owed it to him or not. But then I quickly pushed that thought from my mind. I needed a break from Colten and my thoughts that swirled when he was close.

Taking the afternoon to spend time with Abigail sounded heavenly. And then, when I came back to face Colten, I would be ready to take on any of the feelings that crept up.

Hopefully, I would manage to convince myself that I didn't have feelings for Colten and that I was madly in love with Walker. That my life would be happiest spent here, not in Magnolia with Colten by my side.

Even though I doubted those thoughts as they entered my mind, I shrugged off the fear. I was going to be okay with Walker. I really was. Even if I had to make myself be okay, I was going to find the way.

Certainty with Walker trumped uncertainty with

Colten. And right now, I needed the certainty. Or I was going to break.

And once I was broken, I was certain there was no way to fix me.

Ever.

13

PENNY

My eyes were swollen when I woke up the next morning. Thankfully, Spencer was gone, so he wasn't around to witness my mess. I stood in front of the mirror in the bathroom, pressing into the bags that seemed packed and ready for a vacation.

I groaned as I flipped on the faucet and ran my fingers underneath the cold water. The sharp temperature helped wake me up more. After filling my hands a few times, letting the water run through my fingers, I leaned forward and splashed my face.

I sucked in a sharp breath as tiny needles stabbed my skin. After a few splashes, I grabbed the nearby towel and blotted my face. Thankfully, the cool water helped alleviate my swollen eyes. Once my hair was brushed and my makeup was on, I no longer looked like death.

I dressed and milled around the room for about an

hour before I grabbed my purse and phone and slipped on my shoes. There was no way I was going to be able to wait for Spencer to come back. I was going to go insane if I did.

I needed something to distract me. Even though I didn't want to spend more time with her, I'd take Missy and her demands over loneliness any day.

I locked our room and headed downstairs. I could hear voices conversing, and for a moment, I hoped that I would see Spencer when I finally descended, but that hope was unrealized.

Missy was sitting at the table with her son and his friend. They were eating and talking with the occasional laugh. I hoped that I could slip out, unseen, but Missy seemed to be as alert as a bomb-sniffing dog. Her gaze was instantly on me.

"You're finally awake," she said as she stood up from the table. I wanted to tell her that I would get food in town, but she was already dishing me up a plate before the words formed in my mouth.

Realizing that there was no way I was going to leave without disappointing my host, I settled down on the chair across from Jack and William. Jack was giving me a sympathetic smile, and William was busy eating sausage gravy and biscuits. Honestly, seeing the food was making me glad Missy forced me to stay.

"It's best to just go along," Jack said, leaning toward me in an effort to keep his mother from hearing.

"I'm learning that," I said as I poured myself a glass of water from the pitcher on the table.

Jack didn't have time to respond before Missy was back with my plate. She'd piled so much food onto it, and I had no idea how she thought I would be able to eat it all. From my interactions with Missy, this was becoming the norm. She didn't do things small.

We ate in silence. I wasn't sure I had the self-control to stop myself from inhaling the food. The stress of this trip had taken its toll on me, and I was medicating myself with food. I knew I'd regret it when I got back to Magnolia. I feared the havoc it would wreck on my waistline, but that would be future Penny's problem. Right now, I was determined to focus on keeping my personal life in order.

Once my plate was cleared, I glanced up to catch Missy watching me. Her expression was a peculiar one, as if she were trying to solve a riddle. Worried that she would ask me about Spencer, I gave her a quick smile and pushed my plate to the center of the table.

"That was delicious," I said as I moved to stand. "I should get going though. Spencer wanted me to meet him in town this morning." I gave the table's occupants a smile.

Jack and William returned it, but Missy stayed vigilant. She was onto something, and I could tell there really wasn't anything that would take her off the scent.

"Spencer left this morning before I even had the coffee on," she said as she slowly lowered her hand from her chin to the table. She drummed her fingers a few times. "For a couple on vacation, you two aren't spending that much time together."

"Ma," Jack said under his breath as he gave me a sympathetic smile.

Missy waved him away. "I'm not being nosy. I'm just making an observation."

I nodded, hoping they wouldn't see the panic in my gaze or hear it on my lips. The last thing I needed was someone making a big deal out of how Spencer was acting.

"That's Spencer. He needs his alone time. And I'm okay with that. I need my alone time as well." My smile was so forced that it hurt my cheek muscles. But I kept it up. I feared what she would say if I let it slip. "We're not young kids anymore. We don't have to be together to make our relationship work."

"See, Ma? They're fine. They have their things, and that's good." Jack nudged Missy's arm with his elbow. "They don't need you meddling in their business."

Missy studied me and then sighed. "I guess so."

Taking this as my moment to leave, I clutched my purse to my side and hurried out of the room. I didn't stop until I was down the street and had rounded the corner. When the B&B was out of view, I let go of the breath I'd been holding. I tucked my hair behind my ear as tears formed in my eyes.

If our crumbling relationship was evident to Missy, it had reached critical mass. Spencer wanted to spend more time away from me than near me. Was this our future?

Him disappearing and me waiting at home for him to return? My heart was breaking, and it was taking all of my control not to lose my mind here in the middle of downtown Harmony Island.

I wasn't really paying attention to where I was going until a car horn blared next to me. I startled and looked over to see a particularly angry older woman waving her hand at me. I glanced around to see that I was in the middle of the crosswalk and the light had turned green.

I nodded an apology and then hurried to the other side. Just as I hopped up onto the curb, I nearly ran into Abigail. She was holding a large brown bag and looked as forlorn as I felt.

"Are you okay?" she asked as her gaze followed the yellow Volkswagen Bug that honked at me. "Mrs. Vallen has quite a bite. She's honking her horn like she has somewhere to be, when in reality, all she does is drive around for a half an hour before she heads home to feed her cats." She paused and looked me in the eye. "Did you catch my emphasis on cats?"

I nodded as I clung to my purse. I was only half listening. My mind was swirling with thoughts of Spencer and Abigail. Had he gone to see her? Did she know who I was? How long was I going to be able to keep up this charade?

I wanted to come clean. I did, but I liked Abigail. She was sweet and reminded me of Maggie. With the way I was feeling, a little glimpse of home was exactly what I needed. It was selfish, but I wanted to keep this going.

"Where are you headed?" I asked as I glanced both directions.

"To the bookstore. I picked up some cookies for the cafe, but I fear that I will have eaten them all before I get there." She handed the bag to me. "Do you mind carrying it, if you don't have a place to be?"

Grateful for a job, I took the bag. "Sure. I don't have anywhere to be."

Abigail smiled, and we started walking down the street side by side. We were quiet for about a minute before curiosity got the better of me and I spoke.

"Did you have a rough morning?" I asked, keeping my gaze forward, hoping that it didn't look like I was too eager to hear the answer.

"Not particularly, although I do fear I will have a rough week."

Because of Spencer? "Really? Why do you say that?" Was that too nosy? Was I pushing my luck here?

She sighed. "My past has suddenly reappeared."

So, it was because of Spencer. "Is that a bad thing?"

She was quiet, and I feared I'd gone too far. I peeked over at her to see that she'd kept her gaze forward. "I don't know." She sighed. "How do you know?"

I frowned. "About what?"

"If someone will hurt you again."

My throat tightened at her question. I knew the fear that came from not being able to trust someone after they hurt you. But I'd also been the one doing the hurting as well. "I don't think you can ever truly know," I whispered.

Abigail glanced over at me. I could see the pain in her gaze, and I wanted to take it away. As much as I didn't want to admit it, I was starting to see Abigail as my own daughter. There was so much that I wanted to do for her, which only made my heart ache more. If Spencer left me, I was certain I would break.

"That's my fear."

I nodded. I understood. "And that's a natural fear." I sighed as I let my thoughts percolate before I spoke again. "The truth is, there is so much in this world that we have to take on faith." I nodded toward the sun shining above us. "We have to believe that the sun will rise every morning, or we would never go to bed at night. We have to believe that the earth will keep turning, or we would cease to desire to live."

I gave her a sympathetic smile. Her expression had softened, and I could tell that she was taking in what I was saying.

"If the person is making an effort to reach out to you, although it's scary, sometimes we need to take a step forward." I paused as the realization of what Maggie had gone through washed over me. "I'm glad my daughter did that for me."

Abigail nodded, but a moment later she stopped. "How did you know that it was my dad?"

I paused and turned to look at her, fearing that my

cover had been blown. "I—um—." I knew that this was the moment to tell her the real truth. To come clean with her about who I was. But there was a part of me that was forbidding me from speaking.

I couldn't lose two people in a matter of a week. Even though I'd just met Abigail, she really felt like a daughter to me. "You told me."

A small part of me died in that moment, but I pushed it aside. I was doing this for Abigail and Spencer. They were going to struggle with moving toward each other if I didn't intervene. So, what if I fibbed a little? A white lie never hurt anyone. Eventually, they would thank me. It was only a matter of time.

Abigail studied me for a moment before she nodded and released a soft chuckle. "Right," she said as she squeezed her eyes shut and shook her head. "It's been a week."

My body physically relaxed. The adrenaline that had been pumping through my veins dissipated, leaving me feeling weak and vulnerable. I didn't like that feeling.

"Shouldn't we hurry these to your cafe?" I asked as I held up the bag.

Whatever confusion Abigail was experiencing was quickly wiped away at my mention of the baked goodies I was carrying. She nodded and hurried down the sidewalk. I had to racewalk to keep up with her.

She mumbled something about an interview. Just as

we rounded the corner to the front of the store, I stopped dead in my tracks.

Naomi was standing outside the door, staring up at the sign as if she were making sure she was at the right place. She must have heard us coming because, as soon as we were in view, her gaze dropped to Abigail and her smile widened.

"I'm so sorry," Abigail said as she fished her keys from her purse. "I got distracted at the bakery and then with Penny." She nodded in my direction.

Naomi glanced over at me, and her eyebrows rose when our gazes met. I gave her a pleading smile as I brought my finger to my lips. She frowned but then turned her attention back to Abigail.

"It's really not a big deal. I've only been waiting a few minutes."

Abigail looked guilty. "That's a few minutes too long," she said as she turned the door handle and pushed into the shop.

The lights were on, and there was soft instrumental music playing in the background. It was as if Abigail had stepped out for just a moment. She dropped her keys on the counter and moved to take the bag of goodies from me.

"Where are my manners?" she said as she turned to face us. "Penny, this is Naomi. Naomi, Penny."

I nodded toward Naomi, who looked completely confused. "It's nice to meet you, Naomi," I said as I extended my hand.

She took it, looking sideways at me. "You, too."

"Penny is visiting for the week, and I just hired Naomi," Abigail said as she hurried over to the cafe counter and began to unload the baked goods onto the trays before sliding them back into the glass case under the counter.

"Oh, nice," I said, giving Naomi a smile.

Naomi looked confused, but thankfully, she let it go. Abigail waved toward the small table in the corner, and we both moved to sit.

"Now, cookie or Danish?" she asked, standing behind us.

"Cookie," I said at the same time Naomi said, "Danish."

Abigail nodded and hurried to fill our orders. When she was out of earshot, Naomi leaned forward.

"What is going on?" she asked.

I shook my head, hoping she would understand that this was not the time or place to talk about this, but she didn't let up. Her gaze remained focused on me.

"This is Spencer's daughter," I whispered under my breath, tipping my face away from Abigail so she wouldn't think we were talking about her.

Naomi glanced over her shoulder at Abigail. "Really? Where is he?"

I raised the hand that I'd been clutching in my lap to tell her to let it go, but she didn't pick up on my subtle hint. I sighed. "I'll tell you later."

That seemed to appease her. A few seconds later, Abigail was back and smiling at both of us.

"Here you go," she said as she set the treats down on the table.

"Thanks," I said as I picked up the cookie. If I was eating, then no one would ask me questions. If no one asked me questions, then I could keep my secret for a bit longer. I feared that if I opened my mouth, I would spill my guts to both of them.

"I have the papers for you to sign when you're done eating," Abigail said as she sat back in her chair.

Naomi was biting into her Danish, so she just nodded as her teeth sunk into the soft pastry.

We were quiet for a minute as we finished our food. Abigail seemed content to just sit there with her arms folded and the music serenading us. Just as I dusted off the cookie crumbs from my fingers, the bell on the door chimed.

We all looked over, and as soon as I saw Spencer standing there, my heart sank. From the tension that I saw building in Abigail's shoulders, she felt just as anxious.

"What is he..." she whispered as she moved to stand.

Not sure what I should do, I stood as well. I feared what was about to happen, and there was a part of me that wanted to stop this before it blew up.

That seemed to be the wrong move. Spencer's gaze landed on me, and a look of betrayal and anger flashed in his eyes. He frowned, the crease between his eyebrows deepening.

"I'm sorry," he mumbled before he turned and sprinted away from the store before Abigail or I could say anything to stop him.

We both remained standing as if we didn't know what to do or say. Naomi was just glancing between us, and I could tell she felt awkward. Abigail finally turned her focus back on us, an apologetic smile on her lips.

"I'm sorry, ladies, I'm going to have to call it an afternoon," she said.

I couldn't agree more.

"I'll come back later," Naomi said as she wiped her fingers on a napkin she'd pulled from the dispenser in the middle of the table.

"That would be best," Abigail said.

"I should get going as well." The urge to sprint from the store was overtaking me.

Abigail gave me a nod, and I hurried out the door. Once outside, I glanced down both sidewalks, wondering where Spencer had gone. When I came up empty-handed, I made a quick decision and hurried to the left. He couldn't have gotten far, and there was a chance that I would be able to catch up with him.

Apparently, I'd picked the right direction. Just as I rounded the corner of the hardware store, I found Spencer. He was leaning against the wall with his hands shoved into his pockets and his head tipped up toward the sky. I lingered at the edge of the building, wondering if I should approach him.

Then, feeling ridiculous, I squared my shoulders and marched over to him. "Hey," I said, hating that my voice sounded so weak. Why wasn't I stronger?

Spencer's body stiffened before he tipped his face slowly down to meet my gaze. His frown deepened as he stared at me.

This wasn't good.

"What were you doing there?" he asked.

I wanted to take offense at his tone of voice, but I honestly couldn't. I knew I'd overstepped both with Abigail and with Spencer. It was a risk, and I'd taken it knowing that I would have to deal with the consequences.

"I can explain," I said as my thoughts swirled in my mind. I wanted them to cease moving and form something coherent, but that seemed impossible right now.

"I don't need you to explain. From what I can see, you went against what I asked. I wanted to make amends with Abigail and Sabrina on my own terms. You..." His voice deepened to a growl. "You didn't honor my feelings."

He was right. I'd been wrong. "I haven't met Sabrina yet." The words slipped out of my lips as if that somehow made up for me breaking his trust.

He furrowed his brow. "That doesn't matter."

I pinched my lips shut, silently scolding myself. What was wrong with me? "I know," I whispered.

"Go back to Magnolia."

I blinked, turning my gaze to meet his. "What?"

"You heard me. Go back to Magnolia." He squared his shoulders. "Leave."

My throat tightened from the emotions that had built up inside of it. I swallowed, hoping to move them, but nothing happened. Every muscle in my body felt tight. "Spencer, I—"

"Goodbye, Penny."

Before I could stop him, he turned and hurried away. I stood there, like an idiot, staring at his retreating frame. I wanted to call out his name. I wanted to beg him to come back. I wanted him to change his mind and to forgive me.

But nothing came out when I parted my lips. Tears stung my eyes as they threatened to fall. My entire body went limp as my greatest fear became realized.

Everything that I'd hoped would happen with Spencer—the future I had planned—disappeared before my eyes.

I was right back to where I'd been when I first moved to Magnolia. I still had Maggie, but she and Archer were trying for a baby. Soon, she was going to be wrapped up in her life as a wife and a mother. Being a daughter was going to play second fiddle.

I wasn't disappointed about that. It was all I wanted for her.

For the last few months, Spencer had been all that I'd wanted for me. And now, that future was gone. It had slipped through my fingers so fast, giving me whiplash and breaking my heart in one fell swoop.

I'd started this trip so optimistic, and now, everything I'd hoped for was gone.

I was all alone.

Again.

14

NAOMI

I lingered around town after I left the bookstore, not wanting to go home. I'd been looking forward to spending time with Abigail and getting away from Colten, and I didn't know what to do with myself when my afternoon got cut short.

It wasn't like Harmony Island was very big. It only took me an hour to wander through each little shop on the way home. I was disappointed when I found myself standing in front of my apartment building. I didn't want to face Colten.

My fingers lingered on the door handle until I felt like an idiot and pulled the door open. I boarded the elevator and rode it to the second floor, where I got off. I fiddled with my keys on my key chain as I walked to our apartment.

Just as I rounded the corner to the hallway that led to

my place, my phone chimed. I paused, ducking into a stair-well, grateful for any distraction to keep me from facing what I didn't want to face.

I pulled out my phone and looked down. It was a text from Walker.

A feeling of dread and annoyance filled my chest. I blinked, startled by my reaction. That wasn't normal.

I swiped my phone on and read his message.

Walker: Come home now

I stared at the three little words. *Come home now?* Why was he texting that? Why did he make it sound like he was home? I wanted to text back, "Why?" but I decided not to. Instead, I shoved my phone back into my purse, hurried down the hallway, and shoved my key into the door handle.

I pushed into the apartment to find Walker standing in the kitchen. His arms were folded, and he was glaring. Confused, I stumbled into the room. "Walker?" I asked, my gaze raking over his body. "What are you doing here?"

His gaze snapped to me, and I could see the anger there. "I came home early." He jutted his finger in Colten's direction. "Do you want to tell me what he is doing here?"

My entire body warmed when I realized that Colten was half standing, half sitting on the back of the couch. His arms were folded, and he looked just as ticked off as Walker did.

"I told you, I'm visiting a friend."

Walker shot him a glare. "I would believe that if you two didn't feel as if you needed to hide this from me."

I approached him with my hands out, trying to defuse the situation unfolding in front of me. I didn't know what I wanted relationship-wise, but I did know that I didn't want a fight. "He's right. He's just staying with me to give my brother a report on what is going on here. That's all."

Walker let me get close enough to lay a hand on his forearm. His gaze snapped down to me again and he frowned. I offered him a calm smile.

"Why didn't you tell me?" His voice had softened, which I took as a good sign.

I shrugged as I stepped closer. "I figured your service would be bad."

Walker studied me. From the corner of my eye, I saw Colten scowl. I thought about giving him an exasperated look, but I couldn't break my connection with Walker until I calmed him down. I could always deal with Colten later.

Walker paused before he took in a deep breath. Then he stepped forward until we were cheek to cheek. "Get rid of him, and then we can talk." His voice was low, and his breath was hot on my skin.

He was gone before I could respond. I was left standing there, staring into the distance as his words washed over me. I swallowed when I realized what he'd asked me to do. The truth was, I didn't want Colten to leave. I was selfish, and I wanted him to stay. I wanted

Walker to get along with Jackson and Colten. They mattered a lot to me.

It wasn't fair that he was making me choose.

I gathered my strength and turned to face Colten. He was standing now with his arms crossed in front of him. His eyebrows were knit together, and I could see his jaw twitching from frustration. All hope of an amicable departure flew out the window as I faced the raging bull in front of me.

I took a step forward and parted my lips, but Colten beat me to it.

He pushed his hand through his hair as he moved toward the couch. "I'll get my things and go," he said, avoiding my gaze as he passed by me.

"It'll only be for a little while," I squeaked out. I knew it was lame, but I couldn't stop myself. I needed Colten to be okay with this. I needed him not to be angry with me.

He paused, and for a moment, I wondered if he was going to forgive me. That he was going to see this situation from my side. Meeting me halfway was what I wanted from him—needed from him.

His jaw muscles twitched again, and I held my breath, waiting for the words I needed to hear. He wasn't mad at me. He was going to wait until I could figure out a way to mend the relationship between Walker and him.

"I love you, Naomi."

My body froze. "What?" I whispered.

He hesitated before he glanced over at me. When his

gaze met mine, all of the strength that I'd built up crumbled to the ground. Fear gripped my body while my heart pounded in my chest. I felt like I was floating and drowning at the same time.

"I thought I would be fine. That I could come here and check on you. I wanted to find you happy and settled." He turned so he was facing me. His hands flexed as if he wanted to touch me but wasn't sure he could.

I didn't know what I wanted. There was a part of me that wanted him to step forward and pull me into his arms, but the other part knew that the man I was supposed to marry—the father to my child—was in the other room.

"I'm with Walker."

Tears formed in Colten's eyes, and he nodded. "I know," he said with a scoff as he glanced toward the window. "I know that I shouldn't want this." His gaze made its way back to me. My whole body tingled from the want in his eyes. "But I can't help it."

Anger rose up inside of me. I didn't know what I wanted, but I knew this wasn't fair. What he was asking... it wasn't fair. "Is that why you came here?" My voice rose an octave.

I needed to be angry with someone, and right now, that person was Colten. He'd come here. He'd confused me. I'd been content before he came here and shook up my life.

Colten furrowed his brow. "What?"

"You drove here just to confuse me? To tell me this

when I already have so much going on in my life?" I huffed as I threw my hands up in the air. "You say you love me, yet you're asking me to choose. You confused me, and you think that I'm just supposed to say thank you?" My hands landed on his chest, and I began to beat them over and over again.

I was hurting so badly, and I needed an outlet from the pain.

He let me hit him. He didn't move to stop me. I could feel his gaze on me. I hated that I could see how much he cared about me through the look on his face.

Exhausted, I pulled away and wrapped my arms around my body. I glared at him. "Why didn't you stop me?"

"Stop you from hitting me?"

I nodded. Did he pity me? Was that what this was?

He shrugged. "You seemed like you needed to hit someone."

I sighed, adrenaline leaving my body and exhaustion setting in. I shuffled back until I could lean against the counter. Colten studied me until a look of resignation passed over his face. He turned and began to stuff his belongings into his duffel bag.

I wanted to stop him at the same time I wanted him to go.

My tongue was tied and my body limp as he pulled the zipper shut and shouldered the strap. He turned to look at me before he glanced in the direction of my bedroom. Where Walker had disappeared to.

He took a step forward. "You asked if you're supposed to tell me thank you."

I frowned. I couldn't really remember what I'd said. This whole exchange felt like a bad dream. "Okay," I whispered.

He shrugged. "Everything I did, I did because I care about you. Because I want to see you happy. I never wanted you to tell me thank you."

"So, what did you want me to tell you?"

He glanced down at his hands before looking back up. "That you could love me too."

His words hit me like a semitruck. I stared at him as he met my gaze and held it. There was so much in the way he looked at me. I felt like I was standing on a bridge, staring down at the rushing water in front of me. I needed to make a choice, yet I didn't want to.

What if I made the wrong decision? I cared about Colten a lot. Spending this much time with him made me wonder if I could love him like he wanted me to. But I had Walker. Walker was consistent. I'd built a life with him.

Colten lingered and then sighed. "I'll be at the Harmony Island Inn if you need me. I'm packing up and leaving tomorrow morning." He gave me a weak smile. "Regardless of your choice, I just want you to be happy. You know that, right?"

Tears stung my eyes, and all I could do was nod. "I know that," I whispered. The emotions that had lodged themselves in my throat felt as if they were gagging me when I spoke.

"Okay," he said. He neared me as if he was going to give me a hug and then changed his mind. He lifted his hand and offered me a small wave before opening the front door and disappearing into the hallway.

Once he was gone, I moved to the couch and collapsed. I closed my eyes and allowed my tears to flow.

The sound of my bedroom door opening drew my attention. Walker came out into the living room with a towel wrapped around his waist. His hair was damp, and his skin glistened from the water droplets that clung to him.

I sat up, quickly wiping at my tears. I cleared my throat in an attempt to put myself together. The last thing I needed was for Walker to realize I'd been crying. I wasn't sure how I was going to explain why Colten leaving affected me this way.

He opened the fridge door and disappeared inside. When he reemerged, he had a beer in hand which he cracked open with one finger. "He gone?" he asked after he took a long drink.

"Colten?" I asked, feeling offended that he referred to my friend in that way.

Walker shrugged as he burped and then took another drink. "Sure, *Colten*."

I stood and glared at him. "I'm taking a nap," I said as I made my way across the room.

"Want company?" Walker called after me.

I shook my head and shut the door behind me. I knew that I shouldn't be this irritated with the man I'd wanted to marry. I should be happy that he was back. If we were going to get married and ride off into the sunset, shouldn't I feel a little more affection for him?

I groaned as I climbed under my comforter and pulled it up to my neck. I closed my eyes, but the only thing I could see was Colten's face as he stared back at me. All I could hear was the sound of his voice telling me that he loved me.

Was that true? Had he meant it? Or was this a game? A ruse to get me to dump Walker? Did I dare believe it?

I turned my face into my pillow and screamed. I was so angry with the men in my life that I felt as if I were exploding. I wanted Walker to be a better man. I wanted him to be caring and kind to me. I wanted him to cook me breakfast and be there to open my door and hold me when I was sad.

I flipped to my back and stared up at the ceiling. The truth—even though it was hard to admit—was that I wanted him to be someone he didn't have the capacity to be.

I wanted him to be Colten.

And that thought scared me more than anything else.

SOMEHOW, I managed to fall asleep. I woke an hour later, feeling groggy and sore. The sound of a ringtone had ripped me from my sleep and was ricocheting around in my head, causing it to feel like it was going to split open.

I pulled my covers off and swung my legs over the side of the bed. Once I felt the floor underneath me, I moved to stand.

"Walker?" I mumbled as I headed toward the bedroom door. Was it my phone or his?

I gently pushed down on the handle and pulled the door open. Walker's voice stopped me in my tracks as his words carried over to me.

"I can't," he whispered.

I stopped. Since when did Walker whisper? I leaned in, positioning my ear so I could hear better.

He chuckled. It was soft and made my stomach twist. "I miss you, too, baby."

My stomach heaved. Who was he talking to? I wanted to scream. I wanted to confront him. But I couldn't move. My body was frozen to the spot.

It was torture, but I needed to know more.

"I'm going to stay here a few nights, and then I'll tell her I have to go onto the rig again. We can meet up in Wilmington." He paused. "She doesn't know anything. Trust me, I'll be able to leave."

Having had enough, I swung open the door. Walker

startled and whipped around to stare at me. His eyes were wide. I was fairly certain I looked like a crazed woman, but I didn't care. I was over our relationship. I was over Walker.

"Get out," I growled as I stomped toward the front door.

Walker shoved his phone into his pocket and hurried after me. As if that was all it would take to reverse what I'd just heard. "It's not what you think," he said, his voice taking on a begging tone.

"Were you on the rig these last few days?" I asked as I dug my phone out of my purse. "Should I call your work and ask them if what you told me is true?"

Walker flinched, but his expression remained stoic. "It's not what you think," he repeated like some lying, cheating doll that continued to have its string pulled.

"It's not? Then what is it, Walker?" I folded my arms. "First, it's the girl on the phone before my accident. Then it's you leaving for a month and not calling me." I waved toward his phone. "Now it's a secret conversation about meeting up again?" Hot tears stung my eyes. I blinked hard to push them back, but it didn't work. "If you're not cheating, then what is it?"

Walker studied me. I could tell that he was trying to think. That he was attempting to come up with a reason for all of this. I knew the answer. He was a lying, cheating jerk, but I doubted that Walker had any intention of admitting that.

Finally, he sighed, and I felt a glimmer of hope begin to emerge. He was going to be honest for once in his life. I braced myself for what he was about to say. Even though it would be refreshing for him to tell the truth, that didn't mean it wasn't going to hurt.

"She's just a friend," he finally whispered.

My heart sunk. He was never going to be honest with me. We were forever going to play this game. I was stuck in a relationship that no longer brought me happiness. I needed to get out.

"Goodbye, Walker," I whispered as I pulled open the front door and waited for him to leave.

I looked at the floor, unable to face the man that I'd given so much of my life to. He'd stolen my happiness and confidence for too long.

"Naomi, I..."

I shook my head. "There's nothing you can do to change any of this. If you ever loved me, just leave." I glanced over to see him studying me.

He was chewing on my words. I could see that he wanted to comply, but there was something he wanted to say and wasn't sure if he should. I hoped the desperate look in my eyes told him to let it go. To let me go.

He sighed and nodded. "You're probably right. I'll get my stuff and go."

For the first time since he'd walked back into my life, I felt optimistic. I waited by the door while he moved around in our room, gathering his belongings. He emerged a few minutes later with his duffel bag slung over his shoulder.

I stepped out of his way when he neared the door. He paused before he stepped out into the hallway. I could tell that he wanted to say something, but I really wasn't interested in what he had to say.

"I'm sorry," he mumbled. His shoulders were rounded, and despite my better judgement, I believed him.

"I know," I whispered. It hurt. All of this broke my heart. I'd given so much of my life to Walker. I was having his child. We were supposed to get married, raise a family, and grow old together. The impact of me kicking him out wasn't lost on me.

I was going to be alone, and that thought terrified me.

"But we're over. It's time we realize that." I mustered a smile.

Walker studied me for a moment before nodding. "Yeah. You're probably right."

I held onto the door while Walker walked through. He lingered in the hallway. "I'll come get the rest of my things later this week." He sighed. "Are you going to be okay?"

My stomach was in knots, and my entire body was tense, but for the first time, I felt cautiously optimistic. I was taking charge of my life instead of allowing others to dictate what I needed to do.

Even though my heart was breaking for a future I was no longer going to have, the sunrise of happiness was starting to emerge inside of me. It was going to take some time to heal, but once I did, I would be happy. Wholly, completely, and genuinely happy.

I was excited for the new chapter in my life.

"Goodbye, Walker," I said.

He studied me for a moment longer before he nodded. "Goodbye, Naomi."

I shut the door and then turned to lean against it. My body felt weak as I collapsed to the floor. Tears stung my eyes. Despite how much Walker had hurt me, I still loved him, and the reality of our breakup wasn't lost on me.

Eventually, I was going to have to tell him about the baby. Walker may be gone, but with this cord keeping us connected, he was never going to leave my life fully. I wanted him to have the opportunity to know the baby. I wasn't so heartless as to keep him away.

But right now, I was going to focus on me.

I was going to do what was right for me.

15

PENNY

Dread filled my chest when I walked into our room at the Apple Blossom B&B and saw Spencer standing next to the bed with his bags packed and his lips pulled tight. I allowed the door to shut slowly behind me before I turned to face him. I'd messed up, but he was taking this too far.

He'd shut me out. What was I supposed to do?

"I'm sorry," I whispered. I wanted him to know that I understood the pain I caused him even though I felt frustrated that he was reacting this way.

He growled. "How long have you been seeing her?"

I sighed as I dropped my keys and purse onto the small dresser. "It didn't start out by going behind you back," I said.

He stiffened but kept his gaze trained on the bed.

"I ran into Abigail on the sidewalk. She invited me to

the bookstore since we both liked the same books." I swallowed, my heart aching for Spencer and Abigail as well as myself. If only Spencer would give up some of this pride he was hanging onto for dear life, we might be able to create a happy future together.

But he didn't seem interested in that at all. Instead, he stood there, his jaw muscles clenching over and over, shredding my already ragged nerves.

"You should have stayed away from her. I asked you to stay away. I told you what I needed, and you didn't respect that." He pulled hard on the zipper of his suitcase and then set it on the floor.

"That's not fair," I said.

He glanced over at me. "What?"

"You are not being fair to me." I raised my hand in hopes that he would let me finish. "I came here to help you, and you shut me out. You asked me to stay away, and I tried. But Abigail asked me to be her friend. I couldn't just say no."

He glowered at me. I could see his pain buried deep in his gaze, but I didn't let it sway me. I was tired of the wall he'd built up, and I was ready to take a wrecking ball to it come hell or high water.

"You should have told me." He folded his arms across his chest, and I could feel him challenge me.

"You're right. I should have told you." Tears pricked my eyes. "But would you have listened?"

He frowned.

"You've been pushing me away since we got here. If I came clean to you about what was happening, would you have even listened? Or would you have reacted this way?" I waved my hand at him.

He paused, seeming to contemplate my words, but then shook his head. "Regardless, you should have respected what I wanted. This is my life I'm trying to fix."

His words angered me. Tears were quickly replaced with rage as I glared at him. "I love you, Spencer. I want to share my life with you. Nothing hurts me more than when you assume things like this don't affect me." I folded my arms and glowered right back at him. "I know you miss Rosalie and that you think you are the only one who can fix what broke when she died, but that's not true. I'm here for you. I want to help you shoulder that burden."

The anger in my voice drifted off, and tears began to roll down my cheeks. Despite the fact that he frustrated me, I loved the man. His pain was my pain even if I didn't want to admit that.

"Keeping your distance keeps you safe. But it's also kept you from the happiness you can only experience when you open yourself up to being loved." My words were a whisper now. Pain had a way of filling me to the point where it hurt to breathe. Hurt to speak.

Spencer didn't look up. He kept his gaze focused on the ground as if he were thinking on my words. Then he sighed, and I allowed myself to hope for a moment that he was finally going to open up to me.

"I know you meant well. I do. But this was a journey that I needed to take on my own." He shouldered his duffel bag and wrapped his fingers around the handle of his suitcase. "And I can't be around you right now."

"You're leaving me?" Was this a permanent thing? Or did he just need to blow off some steam?

He moved to pass by me but paused when we were side by side. "I'm sorry," he whispered, and then he was gone.

The sound of the door latch engaging marked his departure.

With him gone, I collapsed on the bed. I covered my face with my hands and let the tears flow. I was angry with myself for letting things get to this point. I was angry with Spencer for being so stubborn. And I was angry with the world for taking Rosalie from this family and breaking them like it did.

I wanted to fix this, yet I'd only managed to make it worse.

I wasn't sure how long I lay there crying. But eventually the tears dried up. I pulled the comforter around me and allowed my eyes to drift closed.

Darkness had filled the room when I startled awake. I glanced around, hoping for a moment that Spencer had returned. But from the lack of light and movement in the room, I was alone.

I yawned and stretched out. My head was pounding, and my stomach ached from hunger. I was starving, but the last thing I wanted was to walk downstairs and face Missy. I had a feeling she was going to have a lot of questions for me, and I didn't want to answer any of them.

All I wanted to do was pack my things and head back to Magnolia. Being here hurt too much.

My phone rang, snapping my attention over to it. I reached out and turned on the light and looked to see who was calling.

Maggie.

I missed seeing her. I missed being able to meet her for lunch to talk. I selfishly wanted her to come down here and comfort me, but I resolved myself not to act sad or heartbroken. I knew she would hop on the soonest flight and come down here if I asked her to, but I didn't want to inconvenience her.

So, I cleared my throat and swiped the talk button. "Hello?"

"Mom?" She paused, and I held my breath. "What's wrong?"

I closed my eyes. This conversation was already off to a rocky start. She was like a bloodhound when it came to me. She could sniff out how I was feeling no matter how much I tried to hide it.

"Nothing's wrong. I'm fine." I winced at the lie. I wanted to be honest with her—it was a goal I'd made for myself after we mended our relationship—but this wasn't the time to make good on that goal. I didn't want her to worry, and honestly, there wasn't a lot she could do to help me in this situation.

"You're lying to me," she whispered.

I closed my eyes as tears formed once more on my eyelids. "Really, I'm okay," I said, my voice cracking. I cursed myself for being so weak.

"What happened?" she pushed.

"Nothing of consequence. Spencer is just struggling, and I'm trying to be here for him. We're going to be okay." I smiled even though she couldn't see it. In all honesty, it was more for me. I needed to convince myself that everything was going to work out and that I was going to be okay.

"I'm coming," she said.

"Maggie, no—"

She'd hung up the phone before I could come up with a reason why she shouldn't come. I stared at my black screen, our conversation playing in my mind. Part of me wanted Maggie here—I could really use a friend—but the other part wanted her to stay in Magnolia. After all, she had a life there, and I didn't want to disrupt that.

I had half a mind to call up Archer and tell him to stop Maggie, but I knew what he would say. She was an unstoppable force when she wanted something. He had a better chance at stopping the waves on the ocean than Maggie.

Not wanting to think about this anymore, I set my phone down on the nightstand and buried myself in the blankets and pillows around me. I closed my eyes and let my remaining tears fall. I wasn't going to move from this bed until my heart hurt a little less.

The next thing I remember was waking up to a sharp pain in my stomach. I rolled over so I could look at the clock. It was well past seven that evening. I'd slept the entire day away.

I groaned and peeled myself off my bed. My body ached. My heart hurt. And my soul felt defeated. I shuffled into the bathroom and stared at my reflection. Why had I let things get that bad? I should have honored Spencer's wish and just left his family alone. But I lacked faith that he would actually let me in, which was why I'd overstepped and inserted myself into his life.

I should have stayed back. But I thought I knew better.

I flipped on the faucet and let the cold water fill my hands. I cursed myself as I splashed the water on my face, causing my mascara to run down my cheeks. I grabbed my face wash and scrubbed my skin until it turned pink. Then I blotted the water with a towel and hung it on the hook nearby.

I changed into my pajamas, vowing not to go out tonight. I didn't want to run into Abigail or Missy, and I certainly didn't want to see Spencer. I allowed myself to wonder where he'd gone for just a moment before I pushed those thoughts from my mind.

Wherever he was, I hoped he was happy.

I ordered some Chinese takeout from a local restaurant and asked them to deliver to my room. Thankfully, they were used to fulfilling orders like that and they quickly agreed. With my food situation handled, I created a nest on my bed with the pillows and blankets. I flipped on the Hallmark channel, determined to lose myself in cheesy romance and corny one-liners.

With the way I was feeling, it sounded heavenly.

I must have looked a sight. When the delivery driver saw me, his eyebrows rose as he took in my appearance. Not wanting the whole world to know that Penny Brown had had her heart broken, I quickly took the food, shoved the money into his hand, and shut the door.

I hurried over to my nest and dove back into it. I filled my belly with an inordinate amount of greasy noodles and fried chicken. But the pain in my stomach helped mute the pain in my heart. Eventually I fell asleep, and I didn't wake up until there was a sharp knock on my door.

I startled, glancing around to get my bearings. In my haste, I pulled on the blanket, dumping the remaining noodles all over the sheet. I cursed myself as I shimmied off the bed and struggled to stand. My body was cramping from the way I had fallen asleep, and I was feeling my age as I pressed on my lower back in hopes that I could straighten my spine.

The knock came again.

I focused on the door, wondering who on earth was knocking. My heart sank when I realized it might be

Missy. Would she leave it alone if she discovered that Spencer had left? Was she coming up here to console me?

"Coming," I said softly as I limped toward the door. I'd slept weird on my leg, and it had gone numb. It was finally waking up, but the painful tingles made it hard to put weight on it.

I unlocked the door and pulled it open. "Missy, I—"

"Mom?"

I was face-to-face with Maggie. She looked tired but concerned as she stared at me. There was a piece of luggage behind her, and her hair was windblown. Her cheeks were pink as she stared at me and then into the room behind me. "It's worse than I thought," she said, her voice breathy.

"It's okay, Maggie," I said as I tried to block her view. But she'd already seen, and now there was no stopping her.

She pushed past me and into the room. I stayed close to the door as she surveyed my bed. The leftover Chinese food. The TV that was still on, playing yet another Hallmark movie. By the time her gaze returned to me, I wanted a sinkhole to open up and swallow me whole.

"This is bad," she whispered as she walked over and picked up the box of sweet and sour chicken from my bed and closed the flaps. "What happened?"

I swallowed, fighting the tears that formed in my eyes once more. I'd already cried enough over Spencer. I was ready to be stronger. Even if I didn't feel it, I was going to pretend for now.

I made my way over to the bed, cleaned up what I could, and settled down on it. Maggie grabbed the rolling desk chair and pulled it over until she was sitting next to the bed.

Once I started talking, I didn't stop. I spilled everything. I told her about Abigail and how we'd bonded. I told her about how Spencer asked me to leave things to him and how I tried but couldn't. I told her about Spencer finding me at the bookstore and him walking out.

Maggie listened to me. She folded her arms and nodded along with the story. By the time I was done, she leaned forward so that her elbows were resting on her knees. Her gaze was trained on me, and I could tell that she was thinking through what she wanted to say.

"I don't know what to do," I whispered as I brought up my knees to my chest and hugged them. I rested my chin on my knees and closed my eyes as the reality of what my future held washed over me. I was going to be alone. It'd taken me this long to find Spencer; how much longer would it take to find another?

That was if I wanted to find another. The truth was, I loved Spencer. I wanted to spend my life with him. I knew he was hurting, and a hurting person did irrational things. If I loved him like I said I did, wouldn't I want to stick around? To be here for him when he needed me the most?

The pain surrounding me was enough to make me

break. I needed advice from someone, and I hoped that Maggie had a solution.

She settled back in her chair, with her elbows on the armrests. I could tell that she was chewing on her response in an effort to choose her words wisely. "I think you should come back to Magnolia with me," she said softly.

I blinked. "What?"

She gave me a weak smile. "You know the saying: If you love someone, let them go. If they come back, they're yours. If they don't, they were never really yours." She shook her head. "Or something like that."

I nodded. "Yeah."

"Well, I think Spencer needs his time to heal, and nothing you do is going to help speed that process up. Coming to Magnolia will give Spencer the freedom to do what he needs to do. To heal the way he needs to heal."

I wanted to tell her no. If I left, would Spencer ever come back? What if this was the end of our relationship? Was I ready to let it all go?

"But..." I wanted to rebut what she said, but I knew Maggie. Once she decided on something, she was going to stick with it. I had to have some faith in my daughter. After all, she was an outsider in this situation. She could see things differently than I could.

Perhaps there was truth to what she was saying.

"You have to know when to push and when to let go, Mom," she said softly. "I think this is the time to let things go."

My throat prickled when I swallowed. So many emotions rushed through me as I listened to her words. I knew my daughter was wise; I just hadn't realized how wise she truly was. I wanted her to be wrong, but I knew that wasn't the case. She was right.

I blinked a few times, staving off the tears that clung to my lids as well as forcing my mind to accept what Maggie was saying. I was going to walk away. I was going to let Spencer have his time with his daughters, and I was going to have to trust the fact that he would come back.

That he loved me enough not to let me go.

I took a deep breath and forced a smile, just so Maggie knew I was entertaining what she said. Then I squared my shoulders and glanced around the room. "Okay, what should I do?"

16

NAOMI

It was a strange thing, waking up the next morning alone in my apartment. I'd been so used to Walker being around—and then Colten—that when I woke up and was the only person in the apartment, I felt...strange.

It was a good kind of strange. Freeing.

Walker was gone for good. I was no longer going to feel confused or broken about what he was or wasn't doing with random girls. I'd faced that dragon and slayed it. I felt stronger and more confident in myself than I had in a long time.

I loved it.

However, back in the depths of my mind, was the memory of Colten. The three little words he'd spoken to me. The fact that he loved me and wanted me to be happy. He wanted me to be happy with him.

I wasn't sure what that even meant for me or what I was going to do in response.

I shook my head as I pulled off the covers and headed into the bathroom. I took a quick shower and got dressed. I was going to push off any thoughts of the future and focus on the present. Right now, my present included starting my first day at Abigail's bookstore.

I was feeling the pressure. With Walker gone, I was going to need to fend for myself and this baby when it came. I didn't have time to sit back and feel sorry for myself. Time was ticking, and it was up to me to make sure that I was settled enough to care for a child.

I glanced at the clock as I ran a brush through my newly dried hair, my heart picking up speed when I realized that I had nine minutes to get to the bookstore by ten. I was going to have to hurry if I didn't want to be late.

I grabbed a bagel from the fridge and slipped my shoes on before grabbing my purse. I rode the elevator down to the first floor and hurried out of the building.

Thankfully, Abigail seemed to be late as well. She was just getting out of her car when I got to the front door. Her lips were downturned and her countenance sad when she raised her gaze to meet mine. She forced a smile as she slammed her car door and shouldered her bags before hurrying over to me.

"Were you waiting long?" she asked as she pulled her keys from her purse and slipped the key into the lock.

I shook my head. "Nope. We got here at the same time."

She looked visibly relieved as she turned the handle and pushed into the store. I followed behind her as she made her way over to the counter and set her bags down. I glanced around, noting how dark the store was. Once I located the light switch, I flipped it on.

"Thanks," she said as she started up the computer and then moved to remove the books from the bags.

"Are these new?" I asked as I joined her, glancing over the titles.

She nodded. "Retail therapy."

I wanted to ask if it had anything to do with what happened yesterday but decided against it. If Abigail wanted to share, she would do so willingly. I didn't want to talk about what I was going through, and I would offer her the same respect.

"Is there anything I can help with?" I asked.

She nodded. "Yes. You can get things started over at the cafe."

I glanced in the direction she nodded. I wasn't much of a baker or coffee maker, but I would try.

"Sure," I said as I walked over to the counter. Not sure what to do, I started with finding the light switch and then turning on all of the machines. They whirred to life, and for a moment, I wondered if I'd done something wrong. But the noises quickly stopped, causing me to breathe again.

The last thing I needed was to mess up this early.

Abigail must have sensed my nerves because she appeared next to me. She ran her gaze over the machines and then glanced over at me.

"Everything okay?" she asked.

I nodded, but that slowly turned into me shaking my head. "I want to say yes because then you'll be grateful that you hired me, but all this may be a tad over my head."

Abigail laughed as she grabbed a dark denim apron from the hook on the back wall and handed it over to me. I took it graciously, slipped it over my head, and tied it around my waist.

Abigail grabbed a second apron and did the same.

I spent the morning in her shadow. She showed me how to run the coffee machine and how to make espressos. By the time I was skillfully making oatmeal raisin cookies, she felt confident enough to leave me alone. I fought not to slip pieces of cookie dough into my mouth as I worked.

The store smelled like cinnamon and sugar by the time people started rolling in. It became quickly evident that most people came here for the goodies at the cafe. They laughed and chatted as I hurried to fill their orders. Some would thumb through a book while they waited, others would set up their computers on one of the small cafe tables and work while they drank their coffee and ate.

Abigail chatted freely with the customers while helping me keep up with the orders. There were times she would slip away to ring up someone buying a book, but then she would return, all smiles and confidence.

It made me wonder if I was ever going to feel like that again. I was alone in this town, and with Walker and I breaking up, I wondered if I was ever going to feel like I belonged. I liked Abigail, but I also knew that she had a life. To her, I was just an employee. Was I ever going to feel welcome?

Then my thoughts wandered to Magnolia and the sisterhood I'd found there. I'd tried not to think about them, but every so often, they would enter my mind. Fiona, Victoria, Maggie. They had been there for me when I needed them the most.

And I'd abandoned them the moment that lying, cheating Walker came back into my life.

What kind of friend was I?

"Are you all right?" Abigail asked, pulling me from my thoughts.

I cleared my throat and hurried to finish drizzling caramel on the iced coffee I was making. "Yeah."

She glanced over at me. "You're not overwhelmed, are you?"

I shook my head. "Not really. It's nice having you here though. Just to keep me on my toes."

She smiled. "Good. I knew that you would be a good fit here."

I nodded and focused back on what I was doing. I knew she was happy having me here, but I couldn't fight the feeling that this wasn't where I belonged. Abigail was at home here, but I was not. Was I a fool to try to force something that really shouldn't happen?

Was this the adventure I was meant to take?

Luckily, the daily rush slowed to a trickle, and a few orders later, everyone had cleared out. Abigail sighed as she tossed a rag into the sink and folded her arms, leaning against the counter.

"That was a bad one," she said as she grabbed one of the only lingering cookies and took a bite.

"Is it always like that?" I asked as I pushed my hair back and fanned my face.

Abigail shrugged. "Sometimes. Sometimes not. It just depends."

I nodded as I started to gather up the blenders to clean in the sink.

"Do you think you have the fortitude to stick it out?" she asked.

I turned on the faucet, her question floating around in my mind. I knew I had the strength to finish out. After all, I was determined to do what I had to for my child. I just wasn't sure if Harmony Island was the place where I was to stick it out at.

I let the water run for a moment before I turned it off and faced Abigail. She was fiddling with the register.

"Can I ask you a question?" I asked.

Abigail glanced over at me. "Sure."

I folded my arms and rested my hip against the counter. "How do you know when it's time to move on?"

She furrowed her brow. "What do you mean?"

I tucked my hair behind my ear and shrugged. "I guess I've been holding onto what I thought was my future, and now I'm wondering if I had it all wrong from the beginning."

She studied me for a moment before a look of recognition passed over her face. "Did you and Walker have a fight?"

I paused, wondering how transparent I wanted to get with her. Then, realizing that we couldn't be friends if I wasn't honest, I decided to come clean. "The man you met wasn't Walker. It was Colten."

"What?" she asked as she furrowed her brow. Obviously, my response wasn't what she'd expected.

I took in a deep breath. "I told you that Colten was Walker because I didn't want Walker to know that Colten was here."

She narrowed her eyes as if she were trying to follow along. "Why didn't you want Walker to know that Colten was here?"

"Because Walker is my overcontrolling ex-fiancé who wanted to dictate what I did with my life. Who I was friends with and if I could keep my family in my life." Tears pricked my eyes as I thought about what I put my brother through. What I put Colten through.

I'd been so blinded by my desire to keep Walker in my

life that I let him push me away from those I cared most about. Colten would have never asked me to do that. All Colten ever did was make me feel loved and wanted.

"Then who is Colten?" Abigail asked, drawing my attention back to her.

"He's a family friend."

Abigail studied me. Then she shook her head. "I'm not buying it. I saw the way he looked at you. He sees you as more than a friend."

My heart picked up speed. Suddenly, Colten's confession came rushing back to me. "He did tell me that he loved me."

Abigail's jaw dropped. "Shut up. He didn't." Then she shrugged. "I can see it. That boy was staring at you like you were the best thing he'd ever seen."

My cheeks warmed. "He did?"

She nodded. "Which is why, when you told me that he was Walker, I didn't doubt you." She fiddled with the hem of her apron. "Now what are you going to do?"

I hesitated as I weeded through my feelings. What was I going to do? I wanted Colten in my life for good, but would he ever forgive me for what I did? "I don't know." I sighed. "He's from a small town in Rhode Island, and I know he wants to go back there."

"So, you'll be leaving Harmony Island?" she asked.

I nodded. "My brother lives in Magnolia as well." I tapped my fingers on the countertop. "I have friends there."

Abigail furrowed her brow as she leaned in. "Did you say Magnolia?"

I nodded and then realized why she looked so confused. After all, Penny and Spencer were from there as well. "It was coincidence that we ended up here with Spencer and Penny. I never expected to run into them." I tapped my chin. "Although I know Penny better than I know Spencer."

Her eyes widened. "Wait, Penny is with Spencer?"

I nodded. "I thought you knew."

She leaned back against the counter, her jaw dropping slightly, and she looked shocked. "I didn't know."

Realizing that there was more going on here than I was privy to, I decided not to pry any further. Instead, I offered her a soft smile. "I don't know your history, but I do know this. Penny and Spencer are good people. Penny especially. She reached out to me when I first got to Magnolia." I sighed. "I've learned that, sometimes, it's better to put our fear aside and let people in than to live alone."

My own words echoed in my head as tears filled my eyes. All I could think about was Colten and what I'd done to him. I'd used him to my advantage and hadn't taken a moment to consider his feelings. Or how my actions affected him.

"I need to go," I whispered as I started to untie my apron.

"Am I going to see you again?" she asked.

I gave her a hug. "Of course." Then I paused. "But I think I need to turn in my resignation."

She laughed. "I figured."

"Just make me a promise."

She nodded. "Shoot."

"Give Spencer and Penny a shot. You never know where you'll end up."

Her smile softened, but she nodded. "Of course. I'll give it my best."

I gave her one last hug before I grabbed my purse from behind the counter. I pulled my keys out as I made my way through the front door and out into the afternoon air.

Colten had said that he was going to wait around until today. I just hoped I hadn't missed him.

It didn't take long to get to The Harmony Island Inn. I pulled into the nearest parking spot and climbed out. There were only two other cars in the parking lot, and I began to worry that I'd missed my opportunity.

Gravel crunched under my feet as I made my way to the front porch. I waited outside the door before I raised my hand to knock. I took in a few deep breaths and then let my fist fall.

It took a moment before the door opened. A woman who looked in her mid-seventies stood in the doorway. She furrowed her brow before she smiled. "Can I help you, sweetie?" she asked.

I steeled my nerves and then spoke. "I'm looking for a guest. Is Colten still here?"

She glanced behind her and then back to me. "Can I tell him who's looking for him?"

My heart began to pound. He was here.

I parted my lips and said, "Naomi," at the same time I heard Colten's voice say, "Naomi?" from behind me.

I turned, my stomach falling as my gaze roamed over him. He was wearing a ball cap and had his duffle bag slung over his shoulder.

"So, you do know each other?" the woman said.

Colten glanced over at her. "Thanks, Charlotte, for putting me up for the night."

Charlotte nodded. "Of course." Then she laughed. "I was going to tell you I have a granddaughter about your age, but from the looks of things, it wouldn't really make a difference." She wiggled her fingers between Colten and me.

"Yeah, thanks though," he said as he took off his ball cap and did a little bow.

"I'll leave you two to talk," she said as she stepped back and shut the door behind her.

Now alone, I began to panic. What if I was too late? What if he had no intention of forgiving me? What does one say when they need to admit they were wrong?

"Walker left," I whispered.

Colten had turned and was staring out into the parking lot. He glanced over at me in a squinty sort of way before dropping his gaze. "He did?"

I nodded. "I kicked him out. He was cheating on me

this whole time. I overheard him." I scoffed in an effort to cover up the emotions clinging to my throat. "I was wrong about him."

Colten turned to face me. He folded his arms. "He's a prick," he said.

A smile emerged on my lips. "That would be an accurate term."

Colten shifted his weight as he pushed his hands into the front pockets of his jeans. He looked like he wanted to prod me for more but wasn't sure how.

"I love you." My declaration came out so quiet that, for a moment, I wondered if I even spoke.

But Colten heard me. His eyebrows went up as he studied me. "What?" he asked.

I took in a deep breath. "I think I've always loved you, but it was made clear when you walked away from me. I don't want to live without you."

I was angry with myself that it had taken me this long to realize how good of a guy Colten was. "You never left me. You stuck with me when I was stubborn and dumb." I allowed my gaze to meet his. Even though I was terrified that he would reject me, I continued. "I know it might take you a bit to trust me again but know that I'm not going anywhere. I'm here to stay."

Suddenly, Colten closed the distance between us and pulled me into his arms. His left hand cupped my cheek as he lowered his lips to mine. I closed my eyes as a tear slipped down my cheek. I allowed myself to get lost in the feeling of his body pressed to mine.

I wrapped my arms around his neck and rose up on my tiptoes in an effort to deepen the kiss. I parted my lips and allowed his tongue to gently stroke mine.

He growled as he reached down and lifted me up onto the banister of the porch. I giggled but never broke our connection. I wanted to kiss this man for the rest of my life.

I wasn't sure how long we stood there kissing, but when he pulled back, I realized that it hadn't been long enough. I moaned as I slowly opened my eyes to see Colten staring back at me.

I flushed as I held his gaze.

He reached up and tucked my hair behind my ear. "I love you so much." He leaned forward and pressed his lips to the tip of my nose.

"Really?" I asked.

He nodded. "And I was willing to wait as long as I needed for you to figure that out."

I raised my hand and rested it on his heart. I could feel it pound in time with my own. "I'm sorry it took me this long to figure it out."

His hand found mine, and he lifted it up to place a kiss on my fingers. "You were worth it."

I smiled as he leaned back down and met my lips once more. Time felt as if it were standing still. I could have kissed Colten forever. But eventually, the sound of a throat clearing drew our attention over.

Charlotte was standing next to us holding a platter with a pitcher of sweet tea and three glasses. "I'm so sorry to intrude, but I'm worried you'll scare away my customers with this PDA." Her smile was so wide that it was hard to take her seriously.

"Sorry, ma'am," Colten said as he stepped back and moved to take the tray from her.

Charlotte let him have it. As soon as her hands were free, she waved toward the chairs on the porch. "Come on and have a drink with me," she said. "Yours seems like a story that I have to hear."

17

PENNY

The smell of cinnamon and nutmeg filled my nose as I stepped into the inn. Christmas was just around the corner, and I was trying to be happy, but I was finding it hard to celebrate anything.

Thanksgiving came and went, and now Christmas was breathing down my neck. I was still alone.

After my fight with Spencer, he never came back to the Apple Blossom B&B. Maggie convinced me to go back to Magnolia, and she assured me that Spencer would find his way back to me.

I had believed her in the beginning. Now I wasn't so sure. He'd been living on Harmony Island for over a month and had yet to contact me. I was trying to give him his space, but it felt impossible when I didn't even know if he was alive.

"You look beautiful," Maggie said as she passed by me.

She'd been the ever-dutiful daughter since getting back to Magnolia. I wondered if she felt guilty for convincing me to leave. I was certain she could see my pain despite my efforts to smile.

I hated that she felt like she needed to take care of me. But I was hurting, and I couldn't find a way to stop it.

"Thanks," I said as I pulled at the emerald-green turtleneck I was wearing with my dark-wash jeans. I'd made a trip to New York over the Thanksgiving holiday for a little retail therapy. Even though I spent a pretty penny, none of it made me feel better.

Not when I missed Spencer like I did.

Maggie gave me another soft smile. I could tell she wanted to say something more, but before she could, the phone at the desk rang. She held up her finger and hurried to answer.

"Hello?" she asked as she brought the receiver to her ear.

Desperate to distract myself, I leaned against the counter. Perhaps seeing families check into their rooms for the holidays would make me feel better. At least others were finding happiness during this holiday season.

I felt Maggie's gaze on me as her eyes widened. I felt confused. Why did she look like a deer in headlights?

"What is it?" I mouthed.

She blinked as she dropped her gaze. "Of course. I will find you two rooms." She paused and then nodded. "We're excited to have you stay with us." She said goodbye to whomever was on the other end of the call and then dropped the receiver onto its base.

"Why do you look like a ghost just called?" I asked as I pulled a complimentary mint from the container on the counter.

"That was..." She paused.

I turned my attention back to her as I slipped the mint into my mouth.

"Abigail," she finished.

My heart stopped. "Abigail?"

Maggie nodded. "They're coming to Magnolia for Christmas, and they are staying here."

My entire body felt frozen to the spot. "They, meaning?"

Maggie nodded. "Abigail, Sabrina, and...Spencer."

***

Ah! I'm so happy that I finally got to write Naomi and Colten's relationship as it blossomed into something more. The two of them definitely went on a journey together.

PLUS, I can't wait bring everyone back together for a Magnolia Christmas where relationships will be strengthened and perhaps, mended?

Make sure to grab your copy of A Magnolia Christmas HERE!

Want more Red Stiletto Bookclub Romances?? Head on over and grab you next read HERE.
For a full reading order of Anne-Marie's books, you can find them HERE.
Or scan below:

Made in the USA
Las Vegas, NV
27 September 2024

95889027R00132